The Mansion

~ ※ ~

and 18 more Henry van Dyke tales

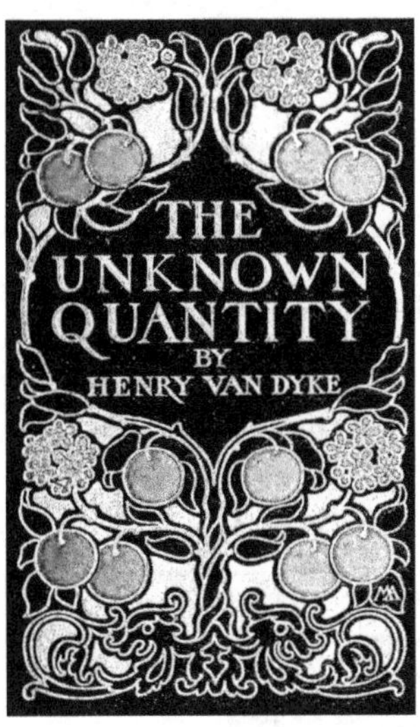

By *Henry van Dyke*

1913 Edition originally published as—
The Unknown Quantity: A Book of Romance And Some Half-Told Tales

~ ※ ~

TABLE OF CONTENTS

"TIME IS" or "KATRINA'S SUN-DIAL"
from Music and Other Poems, 1904

Time is
Too slow for those who Wait,
Too swift for those who Fear,
Too long for those who Grieve,
Too short for those who Rejoice,
But for those who Love,
Time is not.

Dedicated

IN THANKFULNESS

TO THE MEMORY OF

DEAR DAUGHTER DOROTHEA

RAY OF LIGHT

SONG OF JOY

HEART OF LOVE

1888-1912

DOROTHEA

A deeper crimson in the rose,
A deeper blue in sky and sea,
And ever, as the summer goes,
A deeper loss in losing thee!

A deeper music in the strain
Of hermit-thrush from lonely tree;
And deeper grows the sense of gain
My life has found in having thee.

A deeper love, a deeper rest,
A deeper joy in all I see;
And ever deeper in my breast
A silver song that comes from thee.

H. v. D.
Mount Desert,
August 1, 1912.

PREFACE

There is a chain of little lakes—a necklace of lost jewels—lying in the forest that clothes the blue Laurentian Mountains in the Province of Quebec.

Each of these hidden lakes has its own character and therefore its own charm. One is bright and friendly, with wooded hills around it, and silver beaches, and red berries of the rowan-tree fringing the shores. Another is sombre and lonely, set in a circle of dark firs and larches, with sighing, trembling reeds along the bank. Another is only a round bowl of crystal water, the colour of an aquamarine, transparent and joyful as the sudden smile on the face of a child. Another is surrounded by fire-scarred mountains, and steep cliffs frown above it, and the shores are rough with fallen fragments of rock; it seems as if the setting of this jewel had been marred and broken in battle, but the gem itself shines tranquilly amid the ruin, and the lichens paint the rocks, and the new woods spring bright green upon the mountains. There are many more lakes, and all are different. The thread that binds them together is the little river flowing from one to another, now with a short, leaping passage, now with a longer, winding course.

You may follow it in your canoe, paddling through the still-waters, dropping down the rapids with your setting-pole, wading and dragging your boat in the shallows, and coming to each lake as a surprise, something distinct and separate and personal. It seems strange that they should be sisters; they are so unlike. But the same stream, rising in unknown springs, and seeking an unknown sea, runs through them all, and lives in them all, and makes them all belong together.

The thread which unites the stories in this book is like that. It is the sign of the unknown quantity, the sense of mystery and strangeness, that runs through human life.

We think we know a great deal more about the processes and laws and conditions of life than men used to know. And probably that is true; though it is not quite certain, for it is hard to say precisely how much those inscrutable old Egyptians and Hebrews and Chaldæans and Hindus knew and did not tell.

But granting that we have gone beyond them, we have not gone very far, we have not come to perfect knowledge. There is still something around us and within that baffles and surprises us. Events happen which are as mysterious after our glib explanations as they were before. Changes for good or ill take place in the heart of man for which his intellect gives no reason. There is the daily miracle of the human will, the power of free choice, for which no one can account, and which sometimes flashes out the strangest things. There is the secret, incalculable influence of one life on another. There is the web of circumstance woven to an unseen pattern. There is the vast, unexplored land of dreams in which we spend one-third of our lives without even remembering most of what befalls us there.

I am not thinking now of the so-called "realm of the occult," nor of those extraordinary occurrences which startle and perplex the world from time to time, nor of those complicated and subtle problems of crime which are set to puzzle us. I am thinking of much more human and familiar things, quite natural and inevitable as it seems, which make us feel that life is threaded through and through by the unknown quantity.

This is the thread that I have followed from one to another of these stories. They are as different as my lakes in the North Country; some larger and some smaller; some brighter and some darker; for that is the way life goes. But most of them end happily, even after sorrow; for that is what I think life means.

Four of the stories have grown out of slight hints, for which I return thanks. For the two Breton legends which appear in "The Wedding-Ring" and "Messengers at the

Window," I am indebted to my friend, M. Anatole Le Braz; for an incident which suggested "The Night Call," to my friend, Mrs. Edward Robinson; and for the germ of "The Mansion," to my friend, Mr. W. D. Sammis. If the stories that have come from their hints are different from what my friends thought they would be, that is only another illustration of the theme.

Between the longer stories there are three groups of tales that are told in a briefer and different manner. They are like etchings in which more is suggested than is in the picture. For this reason they are called Half-Told Tales, in the hope that they may mean to the reader more than they say.

Without the unknown quantity life would be easier, perhaps, but certainly less interesting. It is not likely that we shall ever eliminate it. But we can live with it and work with it bravely, hopefully, happily, if we believe that after all it means good—infinite good, passing comprehension—to all who live in love.

Avalon,
June 1, 1912.

THE WEDDING-RING

Before Toinette Girard made up her mind to marry Prosper Leclère,—you remember the man at Abbéville who had such a brave heart that he was not willing to fight with an old friend,—before Toinette perceived and understood how brave Prosper was, it seemed as if she were very much in doubt whether she did not love some one else more than she loved him, whether he and she really were made for each other, whether, in short, she cared for him enough to give herself entirely to him.

But after they had been married six weeks there was no doubt left in her mind. He was the one man in the world for her. He satisfied her to the core—although by this time she knew most of his faults. It was not so much that she loved him in spite of them, but she simply could not imagine him changed in any way without losing a part of him, and that idea was both intolerable and incredible to her. Just as he was, she clung to him and became one with him.

I know it seems ridiculous to describe a love like that, and it is certainly impossible to explain it. It is not common, nor regular, nor altogether justifiable by precept and authority. Reason is against it; and the doctors of the church have always spoken severely of the indulgence of any human affection that verges on idolatry. But the fact remains that there are a few women in the world who are capable of such a passion.

Capable? No, that is not the word. They are created for it. They cannot help it. It is not a virtue, it is simply a quality. Their whole being depends upon their love. They hang upon it, as a wreath hangs from a nail in the wall. If it breaks they are broken. If it holds they are happy. Other things interest them and amuse them, of course, but there is only one thing that really counts—to love and to be loved.

Toinette was a woman of that rare race. To the outward view she was just a pretty French Canadian girl with an oval face, brown hair, and eyes like a very dark topaz. Her hands were small, but rather red and rough. Her voice was rich and vibrant, like the middle notes of a 'cello, but she spoke a dialect that was as rustic as a cabbage. Her science was limited to enough arithmetic to enable her to keep accounts, her art to the gift of singing a very lovely contralto by ear, and her notions of history bordered on the miraculous. She was obstinate, superstitious, and at times quick-tempered. But she had a positive genius for loving. That raised her into the first rank, and enabled her to bestow as much happiness on Prosper as if she had been a queen.

It was a grief to them, of course, that they had no children. But this grief did not destroy, nor even diminish, their felicity in each other; it was like the soft shadow of a cloud passing over a landscape—the sun was still shining and the world was fair. They were too happy to be discontented. And their fortunes were thriving, too, so that they were kept pretty hard at work—which, next to love, is the best antidote for unhappiness.

After the death of the old *bonhomme* Girard, the store fell to Prosper; and his good luck—or his cleverness, or his habit of always being ready for things, call it what you will—stuck by him. Business flourished in the *Bon Marché* of Abbéville. Toinette helped it by her gay manners and her skill in selling. It did people good to buy of her: she made them feel that she was particularly glad that they were getting just what they needed. A pipe of the special shape which Pierre affected, a calico dress-pattern of the shade most becoming to Angélique, a brand of baking-powder which would make the batter rise up like mountains—*v'là, voisine, c'est b'en bon*![1] Everything that she sold had a charm with it. Consequently trade was humming, and the little wooden house beside the store was *b'en trimée*[2].

The only drawback to the happiness of the Leclères was the fact that business required Prosper to go away for a fortnight twice a year to replenish his stock of goods. He went to Quebec or to Montreal, for he had a great many kinds of things to get, and he wanted good things and good bargains, and he did not trust the commercial travellers.

"Who pays those men," he said, "to run around everywhere, with big watch-chains? You and me! But why? I can buy better myself—because I understand what Abbéville wants—and I can buy cheaper."

The times of his absence were heavy and slow to Toinette. The hours were doped out of the day as reluctantly as black molasses dribbles from a jug. A professional instinct kept her up to her work in the store. She jollied the customers, looked after the accounts, made good sales, and even coquetted enough with the commercial travellers to send them away without ill-will for the establishment which refused to buy from them.

---

1 There, neighbor, it is good!

2 Well-trimmed, or 'in good order.'

"A little *badinage*[3] does no harm," she said, "it keeps people from getting angry because they can't do any more business."

But in the house she was dull and absent-minded. She went about as if she had lost something. She sat in her rocking-chair, with her hands in her lap, as if she were waiting for something. The yellow light of the lamp shone upon her face and hurt her eyes. A tear fell upon her knitting. The old *tante*[4] Bergeron, who came in to keep house for her while she was busy with the store, diagnosed her malady and was displeased with it.

"You are love-sick," said she. "That is bad. Especially for a married woman. It is wrong to love any of God's creatures too much. Trouble will come of it—*voyons voir*.[5]"

"But, aunty," answered Toinette, "Prosper is not just any of God's creatures. He is mine. How could I love him too much? Besides, I don't do it. It does itself. How can I help it?"

"It is a malady," sighed the old woman shaking her head. "It is a malady of youth, my child. There is danger in it—and for Prosper too! You make an idol of a man and you spoil him. You upset his mind. Men are like that. You will bring trouble upon your man, if you don't take care. God will send you a warning—perhaps a countersign of death."

"What is that," cried Toinette, her heart shaking within her breast, "what do you mean with your countersign of death?"

The old woman nodded her head mysteriously and leaned forward, putting her gnarled hand on Toinette's round knee and peering with her faded eyes into the girl's wild-flower face.

"It is the word," said she, "that death speaks before he crosses the threshold. He gives a sign—sometimes one thing, and sometimes another—before he comes in. Our folk in Brittany have understood about that for a long time. My grandmother has told me. It always comes to one who has gone too far, to one who is like you. You must be careful. You must go to Mass every day and pray that your malady may be restrained."

So Toinette, having tasted of the strange chalice of fear, went to the church early every morning while Prosper was away and prayed that she might not love him so much as to make God jealous. The absurdity of such a prayer never occurred to her. She made it with childish simplicity. Probably it did no harm. For when Prosper came home she loved him more than ever. Then she went to High Mass every Sunday morning with him and prayed for other things.

After four years there came a day when Prosper must go away for a longer absence. There was an affair connected with the Department of Forests and Fisheries, which could only be arranged at Ottawa. Thither he must go to see the lawyers, and there he must stay perhaps a month, perhaps two.

You can imagine that Toinette was desolate. The draught of fear that *tante* Bergeron had given her grew more potent and bitter in her simple heart. And the strange thing was that, although she was ignorant of it, there was apparently something true in the warning which the old woman had given. For jealousy—that vine with flying seeds and strangling creepers—had taken root in the heart of Prosper Leclère.

Yes, I know it is contrary to all the rules and to all the proverbs, but so it happened. It is not true that the strongest love is the most jealous. It is the lesser love, the love which receives more than it gives, that lies open to the floating germs of mistrust and suspicion.

3 Banter.

4 Aunt.

5 Let us see.

And so it was Prosper who began to have doubts whether Toinette thought of him as much when he was away as when he was with her; whether her gladness when he came home was not something that she put on to fool him and humour him; whether her *badinage* with the commercial travellers (and especially with that good-looking Irishman, Flaherty from Montreal, of whom the village gossips had much to say) might not be more serious than it looked; whether—ah, well, you know, when a man begins to follow fool thoughts like that, they carry him pretty far astray in the wilderness.

Prosper was a good fellow with a touch of the prig in him. He was a Catholic with a Puritan temperament and a Gallic imagination. The idolatry of Toinette had, as a matter of fact, spoiled him a little; it was so much that he weakly questioned the reality of it, as if it were too good to be true. All the time he was in Ottawa and on the journey those fool thoughts hobbled around him and misled him and made him unhappy.

Meantime Toinette was toiling through the time of separation, with a laugh for the store, and a sigh for the lonely house, and a prayer for the church. Tired as she was at night, she did not sleep well, and her dreams were troubled by aunty Bergeron's warning against loving too much.

In the cold drab dawn of a March morning it seemed to her as if the church bell had just stopped ringing as she awaked from a dream of Prosper. She put on her clothes quickly and hurried out. The road was deserted. In the snowy fields the little fir-trees stood out as black as ink. Against the sky rose the gray-stone church like a fortress of refuge.

But as she entered the door, instead of five or six well-known neighbours, kneeling in the half-darkness, she saw that the church was filled with a strange, thick, blinding radiance, like a mist of light. Everything was blurred and confused in that luminous fog. There was not a face to be seen. Yet she felt the presence of a vast congregation all around her. There were movements in the mist. The rustling of silks, the breath of rich and strange perfumes, a low rattling as of hidden chains, came to her from every side. There were voices of men and women, young and old, rough and delicate, hoarse and sweet, all praying the same prayer in many tongues. She could not hear it clearly, but the sound of their murmurs and sighs was like the whisper of the fir-wood when the wind walks through it.

She was bewildered and frightened. Part of going to church means having people that you know near you. Her heart fluttered with a vague terror, and she sank into the first seat by the door.

She could not see the face of the priest at the altar. His voice was unfamiliar. The tinkle of the bell sounded from an infinite distance. The sound of footsteps came down the aisle. It must be some one carrying the plate for the offering. As he advanced slowly she could hear the clink of the coins dropping into it. Mechanically she put her hand in her pocket and drew out the little piece of silver and the four coppers that by chance were there.

When the man came near she saw that he was dressed in a white robe with a hood over his face. The plate was full of golden coins. She held out her poor little offering. The man in the cowl shook his head and drew back the plate.

"It is for the souls of the dead," he whispered, "the dead whom we have loved too much. Nothing but gold is good enough for this offering."

"But this is all I have," she stammered.

"There is a ring on your hand," he answered in a voice which pierced her heart.

Shivering dumbly like a dog, palsied with pain, yet compelled by an instinct which she dared not resist, she drew her wedding-ring from her finger and dropped it into the plate.

As it fell there was a clang as if a great bell had tolled; and she rose and ran from the church, never stopping until she reached her own room and fell on her knees beside her bed, sobbing as if her heart would break.

The first thing that roused her was the clatter of the dishes in the kitchen. The yellow light of morning filled the room. She wondered to find herself fully dressed and kneeling by the bed instead of sleeping in it. It was late, she had missed the hour of Mass. Her glance fell upon her left hand, lying stretched out upon the bed. The third finger was bare.

All the scene in the church rushed over her like a drive of logs in the river when the jam breaks. She felt as helpless as a little child in a canoe before the downward sweeping flood. She did not wish to cry out, to struggle—only to crouch down, and cover her eyes, and wait. Whatever was coming would come.

Then the force of youth and hope and love rose within her and she leaped to her feet. "Bah!" she said to herself, "I am a baby. It was only a dream,—the curé[6] has told us not to be afraid of them,—I snap my fingers at that old Bergeron with her stupid countersigns,—*je m'en fricasse*![7] But, my ring—my ring? I have dropped it, that's all, while I was groping around the room in my sleep. After a while I will look for it and find it."

She washed her face and smoothed her hair and walked into the kitchen. Breakfast was ready and the old woman was grumbling because it had been kept waiting.

"You are lazy," she said, "a love-sick woman is good for nothing. Your eyes are red. You look bad. You have seen something. A countersign!"

She peered at the girl curiously, the wrinkles on her yellow face deepening like the cracks in drying clay, and her thin lips working as if they mumbled a delicious morsel,—a foretaste of the terrible.

"Let me alone with your silly talk," cried Toinette gaily. "I am hungry. Besides, I have a headache. You must take care of the store this morning. I will stay here. Prosper will come home to-day."

"*Frivolante*,[8]" said the old woman, with her sharp eyes fixed on the girl's left hand, "why do you think that? Where is your wedding-ring?"

"I dropped it," replied Toinette, drawing back her hand quickly and letting it fall under the table-cloth, "it must be somewhere in my room."

"She dropped it," repeated the old woman, with wagging head, "*tiens!*[9] what a pity! The ring that not even death should take from her finger,—she dropped it! But that is a bad sign,—the worst of all,—a countersign of——"

"Will you go? Old babbler," cried Toinette, springing up in anger, "I tell you to go to the store. I am mistress in this house."

Tante Bergeron clumped sullenly away, muttering, "A mistress without a wedding-ring! Oh, là-là, là-là! There's a big misery in that."

Toinette rolled up her sleeves and washed the dishes. She tried to sing a little at her work, because she knew that Prosper liked it, but the notes seemed to stick in her throat.

---

6 Priest.

7 The scoundrel!

8 Frivolous.

9 Here.

She wiped her eyes with the hem of her apron, and went upstairs, bare-armed, to search for her ring.

She looked and felt in every corner of the room, took up the rag-carpet rugs and shook them, moved every chair and the big chest of drawers and the wash-stand, pulled the covers and the pillows and the mattress off the bed and threw them on the floor. When she had finished the room looked as if the big north-west wind had passed through it.

Then Toinette sat down on the bed, rubbing the little white mark on her finger where the ring had been, and staring through the window at the church as if she were hypnotised. All sorts of dark and cloudy thoughts were trooping around her. Perhaps Prosper had met with an accident, or he was sick; or perhaps the suspicions and unjust reproaches with which he had sometimes wounded her lately had grown into his mind, so that he was angry with her and did not want to see her. Perhaps some one had been telling lies to him, and made him mad, and there was a fight, and a knife—she could see him lying on the floor of a tavern, in a little red puddle, with white face and staring eyes, cold and reproachful. Would he never come back, come home?

In the front of the store sleigh-bells jingled. It was probably some customer. No, she knew in her heart it was her husband!

But she could not go to him,—he must come to her, here, away from that hateful old woman. A step sounded in the hall, the door opened, Prosper stood before her. She ran to him and threw her arms around him. But he did not answer her kiss. His voice was as cold as his hands.

"Well," he said, "I come back sooner than you expected, eh? A little surprise—like a story-book."

She could not speak, her heart was beating in her throat, her arms dropped at her side.

"You are fond of your bed," he went on, "you rise late, and your room,—it looks like mad. Perhaps you had company. A party?—or a fracas?"

Her cheeks flamed, her eyes filled with tears, her mouth quivered, but no words came.

"Well," he continued, "you don't say much, but you look well. I suppose you had a good time while I was gone. Why have you taken off your wedding-ring? When a woman does that, she——"

Her face went very white, her eyes burned, she spoke with her deepest, slowest note.

"Stop, Prosper, you are unjust, something has made you crazy, some one has told you lies. You are insulting me, you are hurting me,—but I,—well, I am the one that loves you always. So I will tell you what has happened. Sit down there on the bed and be quiet. You have a right to know it all,—and I have the right to tell you."

Then she stood before him, with her right hand covering the white mark on the ring-finger, and told him the strange story of the Mass for the dead who had been too much loved. He listened with changing eyes, now full of doubt, now full of wonder and awe.

"You tell it well," he said, "and I have heard of such things before. But did this really happen to you? Is it true?"

"As God lives it is true," she answered. "I was afraid I had loved you too much. I was afraid you might be dead. That was why I gave my wedding-ring—for your soul. Look, I will swear it to you on the crucifix."

She went to the wall behind the bed where the crucifix was hanging. She lifted her hand to take it down.

There, on the little shelf at the feet of the wounded figure, she saw her wedding-ring.

Her hands trembled as she put it on her finger. Her knees trembled as she went back to Prosper and sat beside him. Her voice trembled as she said, "Here it is,—*He* has given it back to us."

A river of shame swept over him. It seemed as if chains fell from his heart. He drew her to him. He felt her bare arms around his neck. Her head fell back, her eyes closed, her lips parted, her breath came soft and quick. He waited a moment before he dared to kiss her.

"My dove," he whispered, "the sin was not that you loved too much, but that I loved too little."

MESSENGERS AT THE WINDOW

The lighthouse on the Isle of the Wise Virgin—formerly called the Isle of Birds—still looks out over the blue waters of the Gulf of Saint Lawrence; its white tower motionless through the day, like a sea-gull sleeping on the rock; its great yellow eye wide-open and winking, winking steadily once a minute, all through the night. And the birds visit the island,—not in great flocks as formerly, but still plenty of them,—long-winged waterbirds in the summer, and in the spring and fall short-winged landbirds passing in their migrations—the children and grandchildren, no doubt, of the same flying families that used to pass there fifty years ago, in the days when Nataline Fortin was "The Keeper of the Light." And she herself, that brave girl who said that the light was her "law of God," and who kept it, though it nearly broke her heart—Nataline is still guardian of the island and its flashing beacon of safety.

Not in her own person, you understand, for her dark curly hair long since turned white, and her brown eyes were closed, and she was laid at rest beside her father in the little graveyard behind the chapel at Dead Men's Point. But her spirit still inhabits the island and keeps the light. The son whom she bore to Marcel Thibault was called Baptiste, after her father, and he is now the lighthouse-keeper; and her granddaughter, Nataline, is her living image; a brown darling of a girl, merry and fearless, who plays the fife bravely all along the march of life.

It is good to have some duties in the world which do not change, and some spirits who meet them with a proud cheerfulness, and some families who pass on the duty and the cheer from generation to generation—aristocrats, first families, the best blood.

Nataline the second was bustling about the kitchen of the lighthouse, humming a little song, as I sat there with my friend Baptiste, snugly sheltered from the night fury of the first September storm. The sticks of sprucewood snapped and crackled in the range; the kettle purred a soft accompaniment to the girl's low voice; the wind and the rain beat against the seaward window. I was glad that I had given up the trout fishing, and left my camp on the *Sainte-Marguérite-en-bas*, and come to pass a couple of days with the Thibaults at the lighthouse.

Suddenly there was a quick blow on the window behind me, as if someone had thrown a ball of wet seaweed or sand against it. I leaped to my feet and turned quickly, but saw nothing in the darkness.

"It is a bird, m'sieu'," said Baptiste, "only a little bird. The light draws them, and then it blinds them. Most times they fly against the big lantern above. But now and then one comes to this window. In the morning sometimes after a big storm we find a hundred dead ones around the tower."

"But, oh," cried Nataline, "the pity of it! I can't get over the pity of it. The poor little one,—how it must be deceived,—to seek light and to find death! Let me go out and look for it. Perhaps it is not dead."

She came back in a minute, the rain-drops shining on her cheeks and in her hair. In the hollow of her firm hands she held a feathery brown little body, limp and warm. We examined it carefully. It was stunned, but not killed, and apparently neither leg nor wing was broken.

"It is a white-throat sparrow," I said to Nataline, "you know the tiny bird that sings all day in the bushes, *sweet-sweet-Canada, Canada, Canada*?"

"But yes!" she cried, "he is the dearest of them all. He seems to speak to you,—to say, 'be happy.' We call him the *rossignol.*[10] Perhaps if we take care of him, he will get well, and be able to fly to-morrow—and to sing again."

So we made a nest in a box for the little creature, which breathed lightly, and covered him over with a cloth so that he should not fly about and hurt himself. Then Nataline went singing up to bed, for she must rise at two in the morning to take her watch with the light. Baptiste and I drew our chairs up to the range, and lit our pipes for a good talk.

"Those small birds, m'sieu'," he began, puffing slowly at his pipe, "you think, without doubt, that it is all an affair of chance, the way they come,—that it means nothing,—that it serves no purpose for them to die?"

Certain words in an old book, about a sparrow falling to the ground, came into my mind, and I answered him carefully, hoping, perhaps, that he might be led on into one of those mystical legends which still linger among the exiled children of Britanny in the new world.

"From our side, my friend, it looks like chance—and from the birds' side, certainly, like a very bad chance. But we do not know all. Perhaps there is some meaning or purpose beyond us. Who can tell?"

"I will tell you," he replied gravely, laying down his pipe, and leaning forward with his knotted hands on his knees. "I will tell you that those little birds are sometimes the messengers of God. They can bring a word or a warning from Him. That is what we Bretons have believed for many centuries at home in France. Why should it not be true here? Is He not here also? Those birds are God's *coureurs des bois*[11]. They do His errands. Would you like to hear a thing that happened in this house?"

This is what he told me.

I

My father, Marcel Thibault, was an honest man, strong in the heart, strong in the arms, but, in the conscience,—well, he had his little weaknesses, like the rest of us. You see his father, the old Thibault lived in the days when there was no lighthouse here, and wrecking was the chief trade of this coast.

It is a cruel trade, m'sieu'—to live by the misfortune of others. No one can be really happy who lives by such a trade as that. But my father—he was born under that influence; and all the time he was a boy he heard always people talking of what the sea might bring to them, clothes and furniture, and all kinds of precious things—and never a thought of what the sea might take away from the other people who were shipwrecked and drowned. So what wonder is it that my father grew up with weak places and holes in his conscience?

10 Nightingale.

11 Servant of the woods.

But my mother, Nataline Fortin—ah, m'sieu', she was a straight soul, for sure—clean white, like a wild swan! I suppose she was not a saint. She was too fond of singing and dancing for that. But she was a good woman, and nothing could make her happy that came from the misery of another person. Her idea of goodness was like this light in the lantern above us—something faithful and steady that warns people away from shipwreck and danger.

Well, it happened one day, about this time forty-eight years ago, just before I was ready to be born, my father had to go up to the village of *La Trinité* on a matter of business. He was coming back in his boat at evening, with his sail up, and perfectly easy in his mind—though it was after sunset—because he knew that my mother was entirely capable of kindling the light and taking care of it in his absence. The wind was moderate, and the sea gentle. He had passed the *Point du Caribou* about two miles, when suddenly he felt his boat strike against something in the shadow.

He knew it could not be a rock. There was no hardness, no grating sound. He supposed it might be a tree floating in the water. But when he looked over the side of the boat, he saw it was the body of a dead man.

The face was bloated and blue, as if the man had been drowned for some days. The clothing was fine, showing that he must have been a person of quality; but it was disarranged and torn, as if he had passed through a struggle to his death. The hands, puffed and shapeless, floated on the water, as if to balance the body. They seemed almost to move in an effort to keep the body afloat. And on the little finger of the left hand there was a great ring of gold with a red stone set in it, like a live coal of fire.

When my father saw this ring a passion of covetousness leaped upon him.

"It is a thing of price," he said, "and the sea has brought it to me for the heritage of my unborn child. What good is a ring to a dead man? But for my baby it will be a fortune."

So he luffed the boat, and reached out with his oar, and pulled the body near to him, and took the cold, stiff hand into his own. He tugged at the ring, but it would not come off. The finger was swollen and hard, and no effort that he could make served to dislodge the ring.

Then my father grew angry, because the dead man seemed to withhold from him the bounty of the sea. He laid the hand across the gunwale of the boat, and, taking up the axe that lay beside him, with a single blow he chopped the little finger from the hand.

The body of the dead man swung away from the boat, turned on its side, lifting its crippled left hand into the air, and sank beneath the water. My father laid the finger with the ring upon it under the thwart, and sailed on, wishing that the boat would go faster. But the wind was light, and before he came to the island it was already dark, and a white creeping fog, very thin and full of moonlight, was spread over the sea like a shroud.

As he went up the path to the house he was trying to pull off the ring. At last it came loose in his hand; and the red stone was as bright as a big star on the edge of the sky, and the gold was heavy in his palm. So he hid the ring in his vest.

But the finger he dropped in a cluster of blue-berry bushes not far from the path. And he came into the house with a load of joy and trouble on his soul; for he knew that it is wicked to maim the dead, but he thought also of the value of the ring.

II

My mother Nataline was able to tell when people's souls had changed, without needing to wait for them to speak. So she knew that something great had happened to my father, and the first word she said when she brought him his supper was this:

"How did it happen?"

"What has happened?" said he, a little surprised, and putting down his head over his cup of tea to hide his face.

"Well," she said in her joking way, "that is just what you haven't told me, so how can I tell you? But it was something very bad or very good, I know. Now which was it?"

"It was good," said he, reaching out his hand to cut a piece from the loaf, "it was as good—as good as bread."

"Was it by land," said she, "or was it by sea?"

He was sitting at the table just opposite that window, so that he looked straight into it as he lifted his head to answer her.

"It was by sea," he said smiling, "a true treasure of the deep."

Just then there came a sharp stroke and a splash on the window, and something struggled and scrabbled there against the darkness. He saw a hand with the little finger cut off spread out against the pane.

"My God," he cried, "what is that?"

But my mother, when she turned, saw only a splotch of wet on the outside of the glass.

"It is only a bird," she said, "one of God's messengers. What are you afraid of? I will go out and get it."

She came back with a cedar-bird in her hand—one of those brown birds that we call *recollets* because they look like a monk with a hood. Her face was very grave.

"Look," she cried, "it is a *recollet.* He is only stunned a little. Look, he flutters his wings, we will let him go—like that! But he was sent to this house because there is something here to be confessed. What is it?"

By this time my father was disturbed, and the trouble was getting on top of the joy in his soul. So he pulled the ring out of his vest and laid it on the table under the lamp. The gold glittered, and the stone sparkled, and he saw that her eyes grew large as she looked at it.

"See," he said, "this is the good fortune that the waves brought me on the way home from *La Trinité*. It is a heritage for our baby that is coming."

"The waves!" she cried, shrinking back a little. "How could the waves bring a heavy thing like that? It would sink."

"It was floating," he answered, casting about in his mind for a good lie; "it was floating—about two miles this side of the *Point du Caribou*—it was floating on a piece of——"

At that moment there was another blow on the window, and something pounded and scratched against the glass. Both of them were looking this time, and again my father saw the hand without the little finger—but my mother could see only a blur and a movement.

He was terrified, and fell on his knees praying. She trembled a little, but stood over him brave and stern.

"What is it that you have seen," said she; "tell me, what has made you afraid?"

"A hand," he answered, very low, "a hand on the window."

"A hand!" she cried, "then there must be some one waiting outside. You must go and let him in."

"Not I," whispered he, "I dare not."

Then she looked at him hard, and waited a minute. She opened the door, peered out, trembled again, crossed the threshold, and returned with the body of a blackbird.

"Look," she cried, "another messenger of God—his heart is beating a little. I will put him here where it is warm—perhaps he will get well again. But there is a curse coming upon this house. Confess. What is this about hands?"

So he was moved and terrified to open his secret half-way.

"On the rocks this side of the point," he stammered, "as I was sailing very slowly—there was something white—the arm and hand of a man—this ring on one of the fingers. Where was the man? Drowned and lost. What did he want of the ring? It was easy to pull it——"

As he said this, there was a crash at the window. The broken pane tinkled upon the floor. In the opening they both saw, for a moment, a hand with the little finger cut off and the blood dripping from it.

When it faded, my mother Nataline went to the window, and there on the floor, in a little red pool, she found the body of a dead cross-bill, all torn and wounded by the glass through which it had crashed.

She took it up and fondled it. Then she gave a great sigh, and went to my father Marcel and kneeled beside him.

(You understand, m'sieu', it was he who narrated all this to me. He said he never should forget a word or a look of it until he died—and perhaps not even then.)

So she kneeled beside him and put one hand over his shoulder, the dead cross-bill in the other.

"Marcel," she said, "thou and I love each other so much that we must always go together—whether to heaven or to hell—and very soon our little baby is to be born. Wilt thou keep a secret from me now? Look, this is the last messenger at the window—the blessed bird whose bill is twisted because he tried to pull out the nail from the Saviour's hand on the cross, and whose feathers are always red because the blood of Jesus fell upon them. It is a message of pardon that he brings us, if we repent. Come, tell the whole of the sin."

At this the heart of my father Marcel was melted within him, as a block of ice is melted when it floats into the warmer sea, and he told her all of the shameful thing that he had done.

She stood up and took the ring from the table with the ends of her fingers, as if she did not like to touch it.

"Where hast thou put it," she asked, "the finger of the hand from which this thing was stolen?"

"It is among the bushes," he answered, "beside the path to the landing."

"Thou canst find it," said she, "as we go to the boat, for the moon is shining and the night is still. Then thou shalt put the ring where it belongs, and we will row to the place where the hand is—dost thou remember it?"

So they did as she commanded. The sea was very quiet and the moon was full. They rowed together until they came about two miles from the *Point du Caribou*, at a place which Marcel remembered because there was a broken cliff on the shore.

When he dropped the finger, with the great ring glittering upon it, over the edge of the boat, he groaned. But the water received the jewel in silence, with smooth ripples, and a circle of light spread away from it under the moon, and my mother Nataline smiled like one who is well content.

"Now," she said, "we have done what the messengers at the window told us. We have given back what the poor man wanted. God is not angry with us now. But I am very tired—row me home, for I think my time is near at hand."

The next day, just before sunset, was the day of my birth. My mother Nataline told me, when I was a little boy, that I was born to good fortune. And, you see, m'sieu', it was true, for I am the keeper of her light.

THE COUNTERSIGN OF THE CRADLE

I cannot explain to you the connection between the two parts of this story. They were divided, in their happening, by a couple of hundred miles of mountain and forest. There were no visible or audible means of communication between the two scenes. But the events occurred at the same hour, and the persons who were most concerned in them were joined by one of those vital ties of human affection which seem to elude the limitations of time and space. Perhaps that was the connection. Perhaps love worked the miracle. I do not know. I only tell you the story.

I

It begins in the peaceful, homely village of Saint Gérôme, on the shore of Lake Saint John, at the edge of the vast northern wilderness. Here was the home of my guide, Pat Mullarkey, whose name was as Irish as his nature was French-Canadian, and who was so fond of children that, having lost his only one, he was willing to give up smoking in order to save money for the adoption of a baby from the foundling asylum at Quebec. How his virtue was rewarded, and how his wife, Angélique, presented him with twins of his own, to his double delight, has been told in another story. The relation of parentage to a matched brace of babies is likely to lead to further adventures.

The cradle, of course, being built for two, was a broad affair, and little Jacques and Jacqueline rolled around in it inextricably mixed, until Pat had the ingenious idea of putting a board down the middle for a partition. Then the infants rocked side by side in harmony, going up and down alternately, without a thought of debating the eternal question of superiority between the sexes. Their weight was the same. Their dark eyes and hair were alike. Their voices, whether they wept or cooed, were indistinguishable. Everybody agreed that a finer boy and girl had never been seen in Saint Gérôme. But nobody except Pat and Angélique could tell them apart as they swung in the cradle, gently rising and falling, in unconscious illustration of the equivalence and balancing of male and female.

Angélique, of course, was particularly proud of the boy. As he grew, and found his feet, and began to wander about the house and the front yard, with a gait in which a funny little swagger was often interrupted by sudden and unpremeditated down-sittings, she was keen to mark all his manly traits.

"Regard him, m'sieu'," she would say to me when I dropped in at the cottage on my way home from camp—"regard this little brave. Is it not a boy of the finest? What arms! What legs! He walks already like a *voyageur*, and he does not cry when he falls. He is of a marvellous strength, and of a courage! My faith, you should see him stand up to the big rooster of the neighbour, Pigot. Come, my little one, my Jacques, my Jimmee, one day you will be able to put your father on his back—is it not?"

She laughed, and Pat laughed with her.

"That arrives to all fathers," said he, catching the little Jacqueline as she swayed past him and swinging her to his knee. "Soon or late the *bonhomme* has to give in to his boy; and he is glad of it. But for me, I think it will not be very soon, and meantime, m'sieu', cast a good look of the eye upon this girl. Has she not the red cheeks, the white teeth, the curly hair, brown like her mother's? But she will be pretty, I tell you! And clever too, I am sure of it! She can bake the bread, and sew, and keep the house clean; she can read, and sing in the church, and drive the boys crazy—*hein*, my pretty one—what a comfort to the old *bonhomme*!"

"He goes fast," laughed Angélique; "he talks already as if she were in long dresses with her hair done up. Without doubt, m'sieu' amuses himself to hear such talk about two infants."

But the thing that amused me most was the beginning-to-talk of the twins themselves. It was natural that the mother and father should speak to me in their quaint French *patois*[12]; and the practice of many summers had made me able to get along with it fairly well. But that these scraps of humanity should begin their adventures in language with French, and such French, old-fashioned as a Breton song, always seemed to me surprising and wonderfully smart. I could not get over the foolish impression that it was extraordinary. There is something magical about the sound of a baby voice babbling a tongue that is strange to you; it sets you thinking about the primary difficulties in the way of human intercourse and wondering just how it was that people began to talk to each other.

Long before the twins outgrew their French baby talk the famous cradle was too small to hold their sturdy bodies, and they were promoted to a trundle-bed on the floor. The cradle was an awkward bit of furniture in such a little house, and Angélique was for giving it away or breaking it up for kindling-wood.

"But no!" said Pat. "We have plenty of wood for kindlings in this country without burning the cradle. Besides, this wood means more to us than any old tree—it has rocked our hopes. Let us put it in the corner of the kitchen—what? Come—perhaps we may find a use for it, who knows?"

"Go along," said Angélique, giving him a friendly box on the ear, "you old joker! Off with you, *vieux bavasseur*[13]—put the cradle where you like."

So there it stood, in the corner beside the stove, on the night of my story. Pat had gone down to Quebec on the first of June (three days ahead of time) to meet me there and help in packing the goods for a long trip up the Peribonca River. Angélique was sleeping the sleep of the innocent and the just in the bedroom, with the twins in their trundle-bed beside her, and the door into the kitchen half-open.

What it was that waked her she did not know—perhaps a bad dream, for Pat had given her a bit of trouble that spring, with a sudden inclination for drinking and carousing, and she was uneasy about his long absence. A man in the middle years sometimes has a bit of folly, and a woman worries about him without knowing exactly why. At all events, Angélique came wide awake in the night with a sense of fear in her heart, as if she had just heard something terrible about her husband which she could not remember.

---

12 Rough speech.

13 Old gossip.

She listened to the breathing of the twins in the darkness. It was soft and steady as the falling of tiny ripples upon the beach. But presently she was aware of a louder sound in the kitchen. It was regular and even, like the ticking of a clock. There was a roll and a creak in it, as if somebody was sitting in the rocking-chair and balancing back and forth.

She slipped out of bed and opened the door a little wider. There was a faint streak of moonlight slanting through the kitchen window, and she could see the tall back of the chair, with its red-and-white tidy, vacant and motionless.

In the corner was the cradle, with the children's clothes hanging over the head of it and their two ragged dolls tucked away within. It was rocking evenly and slowly, as if moved by some unseen force.

Her eyes followed the ray of the moon. On the rocker of the cradle she saw a man's foot with the turned-up toe of a *botte sauvage*[14]. It seemed as if the smoke of a familiar pipe was in the room. She heard her husband's voice softly humming:

> *"Petit rocher de la haute montagne,*
> *Je viens finir ici cette campagne.*
> *Ah, doux echos, entendez mes soupirs;*
> *En languissant je vais bientôt mourir!"*[15]

Trembling, she entered the room, with a cry on her lips.

"Ah! Pat, *mon ami*,[16] what is it? How camest thou here?"

As she spoke, the cradle ceased rocking, the moon-ray faded on the bare floor, the room was silent.

She fell upon her knees, sobbing.

"My God, I have seen his double, his ghost. My man is dead!"

II

In the steep street of Quebec which is called "Side of the Mountain," there is a great descending curve; and from this curve, at the right, there drops a break-neck flight of steps, leading by the shortest way to the Lower Town.

As I came down these steps, after dining comfortably at the Château Frontenac, on the same night when Angélique was sleeping alone beside the twins in the little house of Saint Gérôme, I was aware of a merry fracas below me in the narrow lane called "Under the Fort." The gas lamps glimmered yellow in the gulf; the old stone houses almost touched their gray foreheads across the roadway; and in the cleft between them a dozen roystering companions, men and girls, were shouting, laughing, swearing, quarrelling, pushing this way and that way, like the waves on a turbulent eddy of the river before it decides which direction to follow. In the centre of the noisy group was a big fellow with a black mustache.

"I tell you, my boys," he cried, "we go to the Rue Champlain, to the *Moulin Gris* of old Trudel. There is good stuff to drink there; we'll make a night of it! My m'sieu' comes to seek me, but he will not find me until to-morrow. Shut your mouth, you Louis. What do we care for the police? Come, Suzanne, *marchons*![17]"

---

[14] Hunting boot.

[15] Small rock of the high mountain, I come to end this campaign here. Ah, sweet echoes, hear my sighs; By languishing I will soon die!

[16] My friend.

[17] Let's walk.

Then he broke out into song:

> *"Ce n'est point du raisin pourri,*
> *C'est le bon vin qui danse!*
> *C'est le bon vin qui danse ici,*
> *C'est le bon vin qui danse!"*[18]

Even through its too evident disguise in liquor I knew the voice of my errant Pat. Would it be wise to accost him at such a moment, in such company? The streets of the Lower Town were none too peaceful after dark. And yet, if he were not altogether out of his head, it would be a good thing to stop him from going further and getting into trouble. At least it was worth trying.

"Good-evening, Pat," I cried.

He turned as if a pebble had struck him, and saw me standing under the flickering lamp. He stared for a moment in bewilderment, then a smile came over his face, and he pulled off his hat.

"There is my m'sieu'," he said; "my faith, but that is droll! You go on, you others. I must speak to him a little. See you later—Rue Champlain—the old place."

The befogged company rolled away in the darkness and Pat rolled over to me. His greeting was a bit unsteady, but his natural politeness and good-fellowship did not fail him.

"But how I am happy to see m'sieu'!" said he; "it is a little sooner than I expected, but so much the better! And how well m'sieu' carries himself—in full health, is it not? You have the air of it—all ready for the Peribonca, I suppose? *Batêche*,[19] that will be a great voyage, and we shall have plenty of the good luck."

"Yes," I answered, "it looks to me like a good trip, if we get started right. I want to talk with you about it. Can you leave your friends for a while?"

His face reddened visibly under its dark coat of tan, and he stammered as he replied:

"But certainly, m'sieu'—they are not my friends—that is to say—well, I know them a little—they can wait—I am perfectly at the service of m'sieu'."

So we walked around the corner into the open square (which, by the way, is shaped like a triangle), at one side of which there is an old-fashioned French hotel, with a double *galerie*[20] across its face, and green-shuttered windows. There were tables in front of it, and at one of these I invited Pat to join me in having some coffee.

His conversation at first was decidedly vague and woolly, though polite as ever. There was a thickness about his words as if they were a little swollen, and his ideas had loose edges, and would not fit together. However, he did his best to pull himself up and make good talk. But his *r*'s rolled like an unstrung drum, and his *n*'s twanged like a cracked banjo. On the subject of the proper amount of provisions to take with us for our six weeks' camping trip he wandered wildly. Without doubt we must take enough—in grand quantity—one must live well—else one could not carry the load on the portages—very long portages—not good for heavy packs—we must take very little stuff—small rations, a little pork and flour—we can get plenty to eat with our guns and m'sieu's rod—a

---

18 It's not rotten grapes, it's the good wine that dances! It's the good wine that dances here, it's the good wine that dances!

19 A baptism.

20 Gallery.

splendid country for sport—and those little fishes in tin boxes which m'sieu' loves so well—for sure we must take plenty of them!

It was impossible to get anything definite out of him in regard to the outfit of the camp, and I knew it beforehand; but I wanted to keep him talking while the coffee got in its good work, and I knew that his courtesy would not let him break away while I was asking questions. By the time I had poured him the second cup of the black brain-clearer he was distinctly more steady. His laugh was quieter and his eyes grew more thoughtful.

"And the bread," said I; "we must carry two or three loaves of good *habitant*[21] bread, just for the first week out. I can't do without that. Do you suppose, by any chance, that Angélique would bake it for us? Or perhaps those lady friends of yours who have just left you—eh?"

A look of shame and protest flushed in Pat's face. He dropped his head, and lifted it again, glancing quickly at me to read a hidden meaning in the question. Then he turned away and stared across the square toward the slender spire of the little church at the other end.

"I assure you," he said slowly, "they are not of my friends, those—those—bah! what do those people know about making bread? I beg m'sieu' not to speak of those girls there in the same breath with my Angélique!"

"Good!" I answered. "Pardon me, I will not do it again. I did not understand. They are bad people, I suppose. But how are you so thick with them?"

"If they are bad," said he, shrugging his shoulders—"if they are bad! But why should I judge them? That is God's affair. There are all kinds of people in His world. I do not like it that m'sieu' has found me with that kind. But a man must make a little fun sometimes, you comprehend, and sometimes he makes himself a damn fool, do you see? I have been with those people last night and to-day—and now I have promised—I have won the money of Pierre Goujon, and he must have his revenge—and I have promised that Suzanne Gravel—well, I must keep my word of honour and go to them for to-night. M'sieu' will excuse me now?"

He rose from the table, but I sat still.

"Wait a moment," I said; "there is no hurry. Let us have another pot of coffee and some of those little cakes with melted white sugar on them, like Angélique used to make." (He started slightly at the name.) "Come, sit down again. I want you to tell me something about that pretty old church across the square. See how the moonlight sparkles on the tin spire. What is the name of it?"

"Our Lady of the Victories," he answered, seating himself unwillingly. "They say it is the most old of the churches of Quebec."

"It is a fine name," said I. "What does it mean? What victories?"

"The French over the English, I suppose, long ago. It does not interest me now. I must be on my road to the *Moulin Gris*."

"Will you stop on your way to say a prayer at the door of the church of Our Lady of the Victories?"

His eyes dropped and he shook his head.

"Well, then, on your way back in the morning perhaps you will stop at the church and go in to confess?"

---

21 White flour (high class), brick oven baked, settler's bread.

He nodded his head and spoke heavily. "Who knows? Perhaps yes—perhaps no. There may be fighting to-night. Pierre is very mad and ugly. I am not afraid. But it is evident that m'sieu' makes the conversation to detain me. We are old friends. Why not speak frank?"

"Old friends we are, Pat, and frank it is. I do not want you to go to the Gray Mill. You have been drinking—stronger stuff than coffee. Those people will pluck you, do you up, perhaps stick a knife in you. Then what will become of Angélique and the twins? Stay here a while; I want to talk to you about the twins. How are they? You have not told me a word about them yet."

His face sombered and brightened again. He poured himself another cup of coffee and put in three spoonfuls of sugar, smiling as he stirred it.

"Ah," said he, "that is something good to speak of—those twins! It is easily seen that m'sieu' knows how to make the conversation. I could talk of those twins for a long time. They are better than ever—strong, fat, and good—and pretty, too—you may believe it! I pretend to make nothing of the boy, just to tease my wife; and she pretends to make nothing of the girl, just to tease me. But they are a pair—I tell you, a pair of marvels!"

He went on telling me about their growth, their adventures, their clever tricks, as if the subject were inexhaustible. I offered him a cigar. But no, he preferred his pipe—with a *pipée* of the good tobacco from the Upper Town, if I would oblige him? The smoke wreaths curled over our heads. The other tables were gradually deserted. The sleepy waiter had received payment for the coffee and cleared away the cups. The moon slipped behind the lofty cliff of the Citadel, and the little square lay in soft shadow with the church spire shining dimly above it. Pat continued the *mémoires intimes*[22] of Jacques and Jacqueline.

"And the cradle," I asked, "that famous cradle built for two—what has become of it? Doubtless it exists no more."

"But it is there," he cried warmly. "Angélique said it was in the way, but I persuaded her to keep it. You see, perhaps we might need it—what? Ha, ha, that would be droll. But anyway it is good for the twins to put their dolls to sleep in. It is a cradle so easy to rock. You do not need to touch it with your hand. It goes like this."

He put out his right foot with its *botte sauvage*, the round toe turned up, the low heel resting on the ground, and moved it slowly down and up as if it pressed an unseen rocker.

"*Comme ça, m'sieu'*,[23]" he said. "It demands no effort, only the tranquillity of soul. One can smoke a little, one can sing, one can dream of the days to come. That is a pleasant inn to stay at—the Sign of the Cradle. How many good hours I have passed there—the happiest of my life—I thank God for them. I can never forget them."

A crash as of sudden thunder—a ripping, rending roar of swift, unknown disaster—filled the air, and shook the quiet houses around our Lady of the Victories with nameless terror. After it, ten seconds of thrilling silence, and then the distant sound of shrieking and wailing. We sprang to our feet, trembling and horror-stricken.

"It is in the Rue Champlain," cried Pat. "Come!"

We darted across the square, turned a corner to the right, a corner to the left, and ran down the long dingy street that skirts the foot of the precipice on which the Citadel is enthroned. The ramshackle houses, grey and grimy, huddled against the cliff that frowned above them with black scorn and menace. High against the stars loomed the impregnable

22 Intimate memories.

23 That way, sir.

walls of the fortress. Low in the shadow crouched the frail habitations of the poor, the miserable tenements, the tiny shops, the dusky drinking-dens.

The narrow way was already full of distracted people—some running toward us to escape from danger—some running with us to see what had happened.

"The Gray Mill," gasped my comrade; "a hundred yards farther—come on—we must get there at all hazards! Push through!"

When we came at last to the place, there was a gap in the wall of houses that leaned against the cliff; a horrible confusion of shattered roofs and walls hurled across the street; and above it an immense scar on the face of the precipice. Ten thousand tons of rock, loosened secretly by the frost and the rain, had plunged without warning on the doomed habitations below and buried the Gray Mill in overwhelming ruin.

Pat trembled like a branch caught among the rocks in a swift current of the river. He buried his face in his hands.

"My God," he muttered, "was it as close as that? How was I spared? My God, pardon for all poor sinners!"

We worked for hours among the houses that had been more lightly struck and where there was still hope of rescuing the wounded. The Church of Our Lady of the Victories was quickly opened to receive them, and the priests ministered to the suffering and the dying as we carried them in.

As the pale dawn crept through the narrow windows, I saw Pat rise from his knees at the altar and come down the aisle to stand with me in the doorway.

"Well," said I, "it is all over, and here we are in the church this morning, after all."

"Yes," he answered; "it is the best place. It is where we all need to come. I have given my money to the priest—it was not mine—I have left it all for prayers to be said for the poor souls of those—of those—those friends of mine."

He brought out the words with brave humility, an avowal and a plea for pardon.

"We must send a telegram," I said, putting my hand on his shoulder. "Angélique will be frightened if she hears of this. We must tranquillise her. How will this do? 'Safe and well. Coming home to-morrow to you and twins.' That makes just ten words."

"It is perfectly correct, m'sieu'." he replied gravely. "She will be glad to get that message. But—if it would not cost too much—only a few words more,—I should like to put in something to say, 'God bless you and forgive me.'"

HALF-TOLD TALES: THE KEY OF THE TOWER

So the first knight came to the Tower. Now his name was *Casse-Tout,*[1] because wherever he came there was much breaking of things that stood in his way. And when he saw that the door of the Tower was shut (for it was very early in the morning, and all the woods lay asleep in the shadow, and only the weather-cock on the uppermost gable of the roof was turning in the light wind of dawn), it seemed to him that the time favoured a bold deed and a masterful entrance.

He laid hold of the door, therefore, and shook it; but the door would not give. Then he set his shoulder to it and thrust mightily; but the door did not so much as creak. Whereupon he began to hammer against it with his gloves of steel, and shouted with a voice as if the master were suddenly come home to his house and found it barred.

When he was quite out of breath, between his shoutings he was aware of a small, merry noise as of one laughing and singing. So he listened, and this is what he heard:

"Hark to the wind in the wood without!
I laugh in my bed while I hear him roar,
Blustering, bellowing, shout after shout,—
What do you want, O wind, at my door?"

Then he cried loudly: "No wind am I, but a mighty knight, and your door is shut. I must come in to you and that speedily!" But the singing voice answered:

"Blow your best, you can do no more;
Batter away, for my door is stout;
The more you threaten, I laugh the more—
Hark to the wind in the wood without!"

So he hammered a while longer at the oaken panels until he was wearifully wroth, and when the sun was rising he went his way with sore hands and a sullen face.

"No doubt," said he, "there is a she-devil in the Tower. I hate those who put their trust in brute strength."

It was mid-morn when there came a second knight to the Tower, whose name was *Parle-Doux.*[2] And he was very gentle-spoken, and full of favourable ways, smiling always

[1] Break-Everything.

[2] Talk-Sweet.

when he talked, but his eyes were cool and ever watchful. So he made his horse prance delicately before the Tower, and looked up at the windows with a flattering face;

"Fair house," said he, "how well art thou fashioned, and with what beauty does the sunlight adorn thee! Here dwells the wonder of the world, the lady of all desires, the princess of my good fortune. Would that she might look upon me and see that the happy hour has come!"

Then there was a little sound at one of the upper windows, and the lattice clicked open. But the lady who stood there was closely covered with a jewelled veil, and nothing could be seen of her but her hand, with many rings upon it, holding a key.

"Marvel of splendour," said *Parle-Doux*, "moon of beauty, jewel of all ladies! I have won you to look upon me, now let fall the key."

"And then?" said the lady.

"Then, surely," said the knight, "I will open the door without delay, and spring up the stairs, winged with joy, and——"

But before he had finished speaking, with the smile on his face, the hand was drawn back, and the lattice clicked shut.

So the knight sang and talked very beautifully for about the space of three hours in front of the Tower. And when he rode away it was just as it had been before, only the afternoon shadows were falling.

A little before sunset came the third knight, and his name was *Fais-Brave*.[3]

Now the cool of the day had called all the birds to their even-song, and the flowers in the garden were yielding up their sweetness to the air, and through the wood Twilight was walking with silent steps.

So the knight looked well at the Tower, and saw that all the windows were open, though the door was shut, and on the grass before it lay a jewelled veil. And after a while of looking and waiting and thinking and wondering, he got down from his horse, and took off the saddle and bridle, and let him go free to wander and browse in the wood. Then the knight sat down on a little green knoll before the Tower, and made himself comfortable, as one who had a thought of continuing in that place for a certain time.

And after the sun was set, when the longest shadows flowed into dusk, the lady came walking out of the wood toward the Tower. She was lightly singing to herself a song of dreams. Her face was uncovered, and the gold of her hair was clear as the little floating clouds high in the West, and her eyes were like stars. When the knight saw her he stood up and could say nothing. But all the more he looked at her, and wondered, and his thoughts were written in his face as if they stood in an open book.

Long time they looked at each other thus; and then the lady held out her hand with a key in it.

"What will you do with this key?" said she, "if I give it to you?"

"Is it the key of your Tower?" said he.

"Ay!" said she.

"I will give it back to you," said he, "until it pleases you to open the door."

"It is yours," said she.

[3] Make-Brave.

HALF-TOLD TALES: THE RIPENING OF THE FRUIT

The righteousness of Puramitra was notorious, and it was evident to all that he had immense faith in his gods. He was as strict in the performance of his devotions as in the payment of his debts, nor was there any altar, whether of Brahma, or of Vishnu, or of Shiva, at which he failed to offer both prayers and gifts. He observed the rules of religion and of business with admirable regularity, and enjoyed the reputation of one whose conduct was above reproach.

But, being a self-contained man, he had not the love of the little children of the village, to whom he often gave sweetmeats and toys; and being a very prosperous man, he was not without rivals and detractors, who liked his prosperity the less the more they marvelled at it. This was displeasing to Puramitra, though he thought it beneath him to show it.

"If all were known!" said some people, wagging their heads sagely, as if they were full of secret and discreditable information.

"If we only had his luck," said others, sighing.

But when Puramitra heard of these things he said, "The fruits of earth ripen by the will of Heaven and the harvest is on the lap of the gods."

So saying, he made the sign of reverence, and went his way calmly to a certain place in his garden, where he was accustomed to practise the virtue of meditation and to review his inmost thoughts.

Now the inmost thoughts of Puramitra were in the shape of wishes and strong desires; for which reason, being a religious man, he often called them prayers. They were concerned chiefly with himself. And next to that, with two others: Indranu, his friend, and Vishnamorsu, his enemy.

But the motions of friendship are quiet and slow, and much the same from day to day; whereas the motions of hatred are quick and stirring, and changeful as the colors on a serpent. So Puramitra came to think less and less of his friend, and more and more of his enemy. Every day he returned at sundown to the retired place in the garden, where an orange-tree shaded his favourite seat with thick, glossy leaves, and surrendered himself to those meditations in which his desires were laid bare to his gods.

At first he gave a thought to Indranu, who had helped him, and served him, and always spoken well of him; and this thought he called love. Then he gave many thoughts to Vishnamorsu, who had opposed him, and thwarted him, and mocked him with bitter words and laughter; and these thoughts he called just indignation. He reflected upon the many misdeeds and offences of his enemy with a grave and serious passion. He considered curiously the various punishments which these misdemeanours must merit at the hand of Heaven, such as poverty and pain and disgrace and death, and, after that, all the thirty-nine degrees of damnation; he turned them over in his mind like a hollow ball with rings carved within it, and they played one into another smoothly and intricately, and at the centre of the rings a little black figure with the face of Vishnamorsu writhed and twisted.

While Puramitra meditated thus upon the justice of the gods and the ill-deserts of his enemy, the tree grew and flourished above him from week to month and from month to year, spreading out its arms to hide and befriend his devotions. The white flowers bloomed and faded with heavy fragrance. The pale-green fruits formed and fell from the tree before their time. But of all their many promises one persisted, clinging to the lowest bough, rounding and ripening among the dark leaves with strange flame and lustre—a fiery globe, intense and perfect as Puramitra's thought of his enemy.

"You meditate much, my son," said a Brahman who knew him well and sometimes visited his garden.

"Holy one," he answered, "I pray."

"For what?" asked the Brahman.

"That the divine will may be done in all ways and upon all things," replied Puramitra.

"Then why have you been at pains to poison your tree?" asked the Brahman.

"I did not know," said the man, "that I had done anything to the tree."

"Look," said the Brahman, and he touched the fruit with the end of his staff. A drop oozed from the saffron globe, red as blood; and where it fell the grass withered as if a flame had scorched it. Then the heart of Puramitra leaped up within him, for he knew that his inmost thoughts had passed into the course of nature and fructified upon the tree.

"Most excellent Brahman," said he, with great humility, "the fruits of earth ripen by the will of Heaven."

"For whom is this one intended?" asked the Brahman.

"Holiness," said Puramitra, "it is on the lap of, the gods."

So the Brahman pursued his way, and Puramitra his meditations.

The next day he ordered an open path made through his gardens for the pleasure and comfort of the neighbours. The glistening fruit hung above the path, ripe and ruddy.

"It is on the lap of the gods," thought Puramitra; "if the evil-doer stretches forth his hand to it, the justice of Heaven will appear." So he hid among the bushes at nightfall, and expected the event.

A man crept slowly along the path and stayed beneath the tree. His face was concealed by a cloak; but the watcher said, "I shall know him by his actions, for my enemy will not respect that which is mine." Now the man was thinking shame and scorn of the rich owner of the garden, and despising the prosperity of wiles and wickedness. So he hated and contemned the fruit, saying to himself, "God forbid that I should touch anything that belongs to the wretch Puramitra." And the path grew darker.

Soon after came another man, walking with uncovered head, but his face could not be discerned because of the shadow. And the watcher said, "Now we shall see what the gods intend." The man went freely and easily, without a care, and when he came to the fruit he put out his hand and took it, saying to himself, "The benevolent Puramitra will be glad that I should have this, for he is good to all his friends." So he ate of the fruit, and fell at the foot of the tree.

Then Puramitra came running, and lifted up the dead man, and looked upon his face. And it was the face of his friend, the well-beloved Indranu.

So Puramitra wept aloud, and tore his hair, and his heart went black within him. And Vishnamorsu, returning through the garden by another path, heard the lamentable noise, and came near, and laughed. But the Brahman, passing homeward, looked upon the three, and said, "The ways of the gods are secret; but the happiest of these is Indranu."

HALF-TOLD TALES: THE KING'S JEWEL

There was an outcry at the door of the king's great hall, and suddenly a confusion arose. The guards ran thither swiftly, and the people were crowded together, pushing and thrusting as if to withhold some intruder. Out of the tumult came a strong voice shouting, "I will come in! I must see the false king!" But other voices cried, "Not so—you are mad—you shall not come in thus!"

Then the king said, "Let him come in as he will!"

So the confusion fell apart, and the hall was very still, and a man in battered armour stumbled through the silence and stood in front of the throne. He was breathing hard, for he was weary and angry and afraid, and the sobbing of his breath shook him from head to foot. But his anger was stronger than his weariness and his fear, so he lifted his eyes hardily and looked the king in the face.

It was like the face of a mountain, very calm and very high, but not unkind. When the man saw it clearly he knew that he was looking at the true king; but his anger was not quenched, and he stood stiff, with drawn brows, until the king said, "Speak!"

For answer the man drew from his breast a golden chain, at the end of which was a jewel set with a great blue stone. He looked at it for a moment with scorn, as one who had a grievance. Then he threw it down on the steps of the throne, and turned on his heel to go.

"Stay," said the king. "Whose is this jewel?"

"I thought it to be yours," said the man.

"Where did you get it?" asked the king.

"From an old servant of yours," answered the man. "He gave it to me when I was but a lad, and told me it came from the king—it was the blue stone of the Truth, perfect and priceless. Therefore I must keep it as the apple of mine eye, and bring it back to the king perfect and unbroken."

"And you have done this?" said the king.

"Yes and no," answered the man.

"Divide your answer," said the king. "First, the *yes*."

The man delayed a moment before he spoke. Then his words came slow and firm as if they were measured and weighed in his mind.

"All that man could do, O king, have I done to keep this jewel of the Truth. Against open foes and secret robbers I have defended it, with faithful watching and hard fighting. Through storm and peril, through darkness and sorrow, through the temptation of pleasure and the bewilderment of riches, I have never parted from it. Gold could not buy it; passion could not force it; nor man nor woman could wile or win it away. Glad or sorry, well or wounded, at home or in exile, I have given my life to keep the jewel. This is the meaning of the *yes*."

"It is right," said the king. "And now the *no*."

The man answered quickly and with heat.

"The *no* also is right, O king! But not by my fault. The jewel is not untarnished, not perfect. It never was. There is a flaw in the stone. I saw it first when I entered the light of your palace-gate. Look, it is marred and imperfect, a thing of little value. It is not the crystal of Truth. I have been deceived. You have claimed my life for a fool's errand, a thing of naught; no jewel, but a bauble. Take it. It is yours."

The king looked not at the gold chain and the blue stone, but at the face of the man. He looked quietly and kindly and steadily into the eyes full of pain and wounded loyalty, until they fell before his look. Then he spoke gently.

"Will you give me my jewel?"

The man lifted his eyes in wonder.

"It is there," he cried, "at your feet!"

"I spoke not of that," said the king, "but of your life, yourself."

"My life," said the man faltering, "what is that? Is it not ended?"

"It is begun," said the king. "Your life—yourself, what of that?"

"I had not thought of that," said the man, "only of the jewel, not of myself, my life."

"Think of it now," said the king, "and think clearly. Have you not learned courage and hardiness? Have not your labours brought you strength; your perils, wisdom; your wounds, patience? Has not your task broken chains for you, and lifted you out of sloth and above fear? Do you say that the stone that has done this for you is false, a thing of naught?"

"Is this true?" said the man, trembling and sinking on his knee.

"It is true," answered the king, "as God lives, it is true. Come, stand at my right hand. My jewels that I seek are not dead, but alive. But the stone which led you here—look! has it a flaw?"

He stooped and lifted the jewel. The light of his face fell upon it. And in the blue depths of the sapphire the man saw a star.

THE MUSIC-LOVER

The Music-Lover had come to his favourite seat. It was in the front row of the balcony, just where the curve reaches its outermost point, and, like a rounded headland, meets the unbroken flow of the long-rolling, invisible waves of rhythmical sound.

The value of that chosen place did not seem to be known to the world, else there would have been a higher price demanded for the privilege of occupying it. People were willing to pay far more to get into the boxes, or even to have a chair reserved on the crowded level of the parquet.

But the Music-Lover cared little for fashion, and had long ago ceased to reckon the worth of things by the prices asked for them in the market.

He knew that his coign of vantage, by some secret confluence of architectural lines, gave him the very best of the delight of hearing that the vast concert-hall contained. It was for that delight that he was thirsting, and he surrendered himself to it confidently and entirely.

He had arrived at an oasis in the day. Since morning he had been toiling through the Sahara of the city's noise: arid, senseless, inhospitable noise: roaring of wheels, clanging of bells, shrieking of whistles, clatter of machinery, squawking of horns, raucous and strident voices: confused, bewildering, exhausting noise, a desolate and unfriendly desert of heard ugliness.

Now all that waste, howling wilderness was shut out by the massive walls of the concert-hall, and he found himself in a haven of refuge.

But silence alone would not have healed and restored his spirit. It needed something more than the absence of harsh and brutal and meaningless noise to satisfy him. It needed the presence of music: tones measured, ordered, and restrained; varied and blended not by chance, but by feeling and reason; sound expressive of the secret life and the rhythmical emotion of the human heart. And this he found flowing all around him, entering deeply into him, filling all the parched and empty channels of his being, as he listened to Beethoven's great Symphony in C Minor.

I

There was nothing between him and the orchestra. He looked over the railing of the gallery, which shaded his eyes from the lights of the boxes below, straight across the gulf in which the mass of the audience, diminutive and indistinguishable, seemed to be submerged, to the brilliant island of the stage.

The conductor stood in the foreground. There was no touch of carefully considered eccentricity in hair or costume, no pose of self-conscious Bohemianism about him. His face, with its clear brow, firmly moulded chin, and brown moustache, was that of a man who understood himself as well as music. His figure, in its faultless evening dress, had the tranquil poise and force of one who obeys the customs of society in order to be free to give his mind to other things. With slight motions, easy and graceful as if they came without thought and required no effort, his right hand, with the little baton, gave the time and rhythm, commanding swift obedience; while his left hand lightly beckoned here and there with magical persuasion, drawing forth louder or softer notes, stirring the groups of instruments to passionate expression, or hushing them to delicate and ethereal strains.

There was no labour, no dramatic display in that leadership; nothing to distract the attention, or to break the spell of the music. All the toil of art, the consideration of effects, the sharp and vehement assertion of authority, lay behind him in the rehearsals.

Now the finished work, the noble interpretation of the composer's musical idea, flowed forth at the leader's touch, as if each motive and phrase, each period and melody, were waiting somewhere in the air to reveal itself at his slight signal. And through all the movement of the *Allegro con brio*, with its momentous struggle between Fate and the Human Soul, the orchestra answered to the leader's will as if it were a single instrument upon which he played.

And so, for a time, it seemed to the Music-Lover as he looked down upon it from his lofty place. With what precision the bows of the violins moved up and down together; how accurately the wood-winds came in with their gentler notes; how regularly the brazen keys of the trumpets rose and fell, and the long, shining tubes of the trombone slid out and in. Such varied motions, yet all so limited, so orderly, so certain and obedient, looked like the sure interplay of the parts of a wonderful machine.

He watched them as if in a dream, fascinated by their regularity, their simplicity in detail, their complexity in the mass—watched them with his eyes, while his heart was carried along with the flood of music. More and more the impression of a marvellous unity, a mechanical certainty of action, grew upon that half of his mind which was occupied with sight, and gave him a singular satisfaction and comfort.

It was good to be free, for a little while at least, from the everlasting personal equation, the perplexing interest in human individuals, the mysterious and disturbing sympathies awakened by contact with other lives, and to give one's self to the pure enjoyment of an impersonal work of art, rendered by the greatest of all instruments—a full orchestra under control of a master.

II

But presently the *Allegro* came to an end, and with the pause there came that brief stir in the orchestra, that momentary relaxation of nerves and muscles, that moving and turning of many heads in different directions, that swift interchange of looks and smiles and whispered words between the players, which seemed like the temporary dissolving of the spell that made them one. And with this general but separated and uncertain movement a vague thought, an unformulated question, passed into the mind of the Music-Lover.

How would the leader reassemble the parts of his instrument in a few seconds, and make them one again, and resume his control over it? How would he make the pipes and strings and tubes and drums answer to his touch, though he laid no hand upon them? There must be some strange, invisible key-board, some secret system of communication between him and those various contrivances of wood and wire and sheep-skin and horse-hair and metal (so curiously and grotesquely fashioned, when one came to consider them) out of which he was to bring melody and harmony. How should one conceive of this mysterious key-board and its hidden connections?

How should one comprehend and imagine it? Was it not, after all, the most wonderful thing about the great instrument on which the symphony was played?

While the Music-Lover, leaning back in his seat, was idly turning over this thought, the *Andante* began, and all definite questioning and reasoning were absorbed in the calm, satisfying melody which flowed from the violas and 'cellos.

But now a singular change came over the half-conscious impression which his eyes received as they rested on the orchestra. It was no longer a huge and strangely fashioned instrument, intricate in construction, perfect in adjustment, that he was watching.

It was a company of human beings, trained and disciplined to common action, understanding one another through the sharing of a certain technical knowledge, and bound together by a unity of will which was expressed in their central obedience to the leader. The arms, the hands, the lips of these hundred persons were weaving together the many-coloured garment of music, because their minds knew the pattern, and their wills worked together in the design.

Here was the wonderful hidden system of communication, more magical than any mechanism, just because it was less perfect, just because it left room, along each separate channel, for the coming in of those slight, incalculable elements of personal emotion which lend the touch of life to rhythm and tone.

The instruments were but the tools. The composer was the master-designer. The leader and his orchestra were the weavers of the rich robe of sound, in which alone the hidden spirit of Music, daughter of Psyche and Amor, becomes perceptible to mortal sense.

The smooth and harmonious action of the players seemed to lend a new charm, delicate and indefinable, to the development of the clear and heart-strengthening theme with its subtle variations and its powerful, emphatic close, like the fullness of meaning in the last line of a noble sonnet.

III

In the pause that followed, the Music-Lover let himself drift quietly with the thoughts of peace and concord awakened by this loveliest of andantes.

The beginning of the *Scherzo* found him, somehow or other, in a new relation to the visible image of the orchestra. The weird, almost supernatural music, murmured at first by the 'cellos and double-basses, then proclaimed by the horns as if by the trumpet of Fate itself; the repetition of the same struggle of emotions which had marked the first movement, but now more tense, more passionate, more human, the strange, fantastic mingling of comedy and tragedy in the *Trio* and the *Fugue* with its abrupt questions and answers; all this seemed to him like a moving picture of the inner life of man.

And while he followed it, the other half of his mind was watching the players, no longer as a group, a unit of disciplined action, but as individuals, persons for each of whom life had a distinct colour, and tone, and meaning.

His eyes rested unconsciously on the pale, dreamy face of the second violinist; the black, rugged brows of the trumpeter; the long, gentle countenance of the flute-player with its flexible lips and blond beard.

The grizzled head of the 'cellist bent over his instrument with an air of quiet devotion. The burly form of the player of the double-bassoon, behind his rare and awkward instrument, waiting for his time to come in, had the look of a man who could not be surprised or troubled by anything. One of the bass-violinists had the rough-hewn figure and the divinely chiseled, sorrow-lighted face of Lincoln, the others were children of the everyday. The clarionettist, with his dark beard and high temples, might have sat for Rembrandt's picture of "The Philosopher." The rotund kettle-drummer, with his smooth head and sparkling eyes, restlessly turning his little keys and bending down to listen to the tuning of his grotesque music-pots, seemed impatient for the part in the score when he was to build the magical bridge, on which the symphony passes, without a break, from the third to the last movement.

"All these persons," said the inner voice of the Music-Lover (he listening all the while to the entangling and unfolding, dismissing and recalling of the various motives)—"all these persons have their own lives and characters. They have known joys and sorrows, failures and successes. They have hoped and feared. All that Beethoven poured into this music from his experience of poverty, of conflict with physical weakness and the cruel limitations of Fate, of baffled desire, of loneliness, of strong resolution, of immortal courage and faith, these players in their measure and degree have known.

"Even now they may be in love, in hatred, in friendship, in jealousy, in gloom, in resignation, in courage, or in happiness. What strange paths lie behind them; what laughter and what tears have they shared; what secret ties unite them, one with another, and what hidden barriers rise between those who do not understand and those who do not care! There are many stories running along underneath this music, some of them just begun, some long since ended, some never to find a true completion: little stories of many lands, humourous and pathetic, droll and capricious legends, merry jests, vivid romances, serious tales of patience and devotion.

"And out of these stories, because they are human, has come the humanity of the players: the thing which makes it possible for them to feel this music, and to play it, not as a machine would play, grinding it out with dead monotony, but with all the colour and passion of life itself.

"Why should we not know something of this hidden background of the orchestra? Why should not somebody tell one of the stories that is waiting here? Not I, but some one familiar with this region, who has trodden its paths and shared in its labours; not a mere lover of music, but a musician."

Here the inner voice which had been running along through the *Scherzo* and the *Trio* and the *Recapitulation*, died away quietly with the *pianissimo* passage in which the double-basses and the drum carry one through the very heart of mystery; and the Music-Lover found himself intensely waiting for the great *Finale*.

Now it comes, long-expected, surprising, victorious, sweeping all the instruments into its mighty current, pausing for a moment to take up the most delicate and mysterious melody of the *Scherzo* (changed as if by magic into something new and strange), and then moving on again, with hurrying, swelling tide, until it breaks in the swift-rolling, thunderous billows of immeasurable jubilation.

The Music-Lover drew a long breath. He sat motionless in his seat. The storm of applause did not disturb him. He did not notice that the audience had risen. He was looking at the orchestra, already beginning to melt away; but he did not really see them.

Presently a hand was stretched out from the second row behind him, and touched him on the shoulder. He turned around and saw the face of his friend the Dreamer, the Brushwood Boy, with his bright eyes and disheveled hair. And beside him was the radiant presence of the Girl Who Understood.

"*Lieber Meister,*[1]" said the Boy, "you are coming now with us. There is a bite and a sup, and a pipe and an open fire, waiting for you in our room—and I have a story to read you. *Bitte komm!*[2]"

HUMORESKE

I

They parted at the end of the summer—the boy and the girl—after having been very happy together for two months and very miserable for two days. The trouble was that she would not marry him.

This was not altogether strange, for Richard Shafer was only twenty and had just finished his second year in college. To Carola Brune, who was a year younger, he seemed

1 Dear Master.

2 Please come!

perfect as a playmate, but she simply could not imagine him as a husband. He was too vague, unformed, boyish in his moods and caprices. She was a strong girl, with quick and powerful impulses in her nature, and she felt that she would need a strong man to hold her. What Richard was, what he would be, she could not clearly see. She loved to make music with him—she at the piano, he with his violin. She loved to roam the woods with him, and to go out in a canoe with him on the moonlit river. But she could not and she would not say that she loved *him*—at least, not enough to promise to marry him now.

He took her "no" very hard. He argued the case persistently. There were no real obstacles, that he could see, to their marriage. She was the daughter of a musician, a Bohemian, who would make no objections to an unworldly match. He was an orphan with a little patrimony of four or five thousand dollars, enough to live on until the world recognised his genius as a poet and his mastery as a violinist.

At this, unfortunately, being a little nervous and overstrained by the long pleading, she laughed. "Oh, Dick!" she cried. "Swinburne and Sarasate—two single gentlemen rolled into one!"

Now there is nothing that a boy—or for that matter, a man—dislikes so much as laughter when he is making a declaration of love. His sense of humour at that time is in eclipse, and even the gentlest turn of wit shocks him deeply.

"Very well," he answered, rising from their favourite seat among the roots of an old hemlock tree overhanging the stream, "let us go back to the hotel. I have been a silly ass, I suppose, and now it's all over."

"But why?"—she was tempted to ask him as they walked through the woods. Why was it all over? Why shouldn't they go on being good friends and comrades? Couldn't he see that she had only tried to make a little joke to ease the strain? Didn't he know that she really had a wonderful admiration for his talents and a large hope for his future?

But something held her back from speaking. She was embarrassed and slightly ashamed. He was in a strange mood, evidently offended, absurdly polite and distant, making talk about the concert that was to come off that evening. She could not bring herself to explain to him now. She would do it in the morning when the air was clearer and cooler.

As they entered the hotel, she turned into the music room, saying that she had to practise for her part in the concert. He held out his hand with a little formal gesture. "I wish you a big success," said he; "my part doesn't need any practice." Then he went upstairs to pack his trunk for the six o'clock train.

An hour later, as he passed out of the door, he heard her still at the piano. She was playing for her own pleasure now—just to relieve the tension of her feelings by letting them flow out on the rhythmic current of music. It was her favourite piece, that magical *humoreske* by Dvořák, which is like an April day, full of smiles and tears, pleading and laughter. The clear notes came out under her exquisite touch with a penetrating charm of airy, graceful fantasy. To the angry boy at the door it seemed as if they were full of delicate indifference and mockery. They expressed to him the spirit of a girl—light, capricious, elusive, yet with a will that can resist all appeal and evade all attack—an invincible butterfly, a thistle-down of steel—the thing that a man wants most in all the world and yet can not have unless she chooses. She stood for his first defeat, his great disappointment, his discovery that life can refuse; and now she was playing this quaint, careless, mocking music!

"She does not care," he said to himself, as he climbed into the stage, "and I will not care. She is only a flirt. All girls are like that." With this profound generalisation in what he called his mind, but what was really his temper, he rode sullenly away.

He did not hear how she lingered caressingly over the last phrases of the *humoreske*, playing them very softly, with her blond head bent over the piano, as if she were trying to recall something. He did not know that she put on the frock that he liked best, with the mauve ribbons, for the concert that night. He did not see her lips quiver and the look of pained surprise flash into her brown eyes when she heard that he had gone without even saying good-bye.

Naturally she, thinking him a proud and foolish boy, waited for him to come back or to write. Naturally he, having classified her as a cold and heartless flirt, expected her to send him a letter asking him to return. Naturally neither of these things happened. The little bank-dividing stream of circumstance flowed between them, ever broadening, until it seemed like an impassable river.

Each of them said, "It was only an episode." Each of them was sure that there was nothing in it which could mean a lasting pain, nothing which time would not obliterate. Each of them repeated a wise phrase or two about "passing fancies" and "puppy love," and so they went their ways lightly enough, reasonably resolving not to think of each other any more.

But it was strange how clearly and brightly the scenes of the summer itself lived in their memories. To both of them there was a peculiar and deepening vividness in those pictures of certain places.

The hardwood ridges in the forest, where there was no undergrowth and they could walk straight ahead, side by side, through the interminable colonnade of beeches and birches which upheld the green, gold-flecked roof,—the dark tangled spruce thicket, where one must stoop under the interlacing lower branches, dead and brittle, and creep over the soft brown carpet of fallen needles, dry and slippery, in order to reach a little open glade, moist with springs, where the red wood-lily and the purple-fringed orchid grew,—the high steep rock that jutted out from the woods about half-way up the slope of the Dome, as if to make a narrow view-point of surprise where two people could stand close together and look down upon the broad valley and the blue hills beyond,—the old hemlock, with its big, bent knees covered with moss, ready to hold them comfortably in its lap, while they read poetry or stories of adventure, and the little river sung its sleepy song at their feet,—the long stillwater where the canoe floated quietly among the mirrored stars,—the merry rapids where the moon path spread before them broad and silvery, luring them to follow it down to danger,—the twilight hour in the music room, where the piano answered to the violin, and through the open door and windows the aromatic breath of the pine-trees and the spicy smell of wild grapes drifted faintly in,—a certain afternoon when the cool rain-drops beat in their faces as they tramped home, after a long walk over the hills, wet and joyous, swinging their clasped hands and chanting some foolish, endless song of the road,—a certain evening when the murmuring hemlock above them grew silent, and the whispering water below them seemed to hush, and a single big star across the river was softly throbbing in the mauve dusk, and their lips met for a moment as purely and silently as the twilight meets the night;—these were pictures that would not fade and dissolve. There was something unforgettable about them.

Was it the spirit of place that possessed them with a unique loveliness; or was it that they were illuminated by the charm of a companionship in which two hearts had tasted together the sweetest cup in the world, the royal chalice of the pure, uncalculating, inexplicable joy of living?

Be that as it may, the fact remains that while the boy and the girl went away from each other, and grew separately to manhood and womanhood, and had other experiences and joys and troubles, that summer stayed with them both as something rare and unequalled, set apart in its delectable perfection, a standard by which, unconsciously, they measured all happiness and all beauty.

The effect of such an inward standard is peculiar. It is apt to give a certain detachment, a touch of isolation, to the person who possesses it. And whether that is a good thing or a bad thing depends upon the tone which is given to it by an unknown quantity, the way in which the secret will of the spirit chooses to take and use it.

To Carola Brune it was like the possession of something very precious, which she had found and which she felt she could never lose. She followed the path which was marked out for her as a student of music with tranquil enthusiasm and cheerful industry; she made friends everywhere by her serene and wholesome loveliness; and she did her work at the piano so well that when she went to Paris, at the end of the second year, to continue her studies, she found no difficulty in being received as a pupil by the great Alberti.

"You have a very happy touch, mademoiselle," said the little gray man one day at the end of a lesson. He gave his moustache that fierce upward turn with which he accompanied his rare compliments, and frowned at her benignly while he went on. "I suppose you know that you really play better than you know how to play. What right have you to do that?"

She smiled as she turned around to him, for she had learned to understand his abrupt ways. "No right, dear master," she said, "only perhaps it is because I happen to know a little of the meaning of happiness."

"But you play the sad music too," he continued, "and you let it all come out."

"That is because I am not afraid of sadness," she answered, with her clear brown eyes looking quietly up at him.

His voice grew gentle and he laid his hand on her shoulder. "You have the secret, my child—to know the meaning of happiness, and not to be afraid of sadness, but to pour it all into the music. That is the secret, and it will make you a musician,—it will carry you far, I think,—provided you don't neglect your practising," he added brusquely.

She shook her head and laughed. "I wouldn't dare do that with such a tyrant as you, dear master."

"Next week," he went on, giving a new upward twist to his moustache, "I shall expect you to be letter-perfect with that G major concerto of Beethoven—no more drum-beats, remember. And mind, you are not to think of playing in public, at a concert, until I tell you. It may be a long time,—a year, perhaps,—but I am not going to let them spoil my sweetest rose by forcing her into bloom too soon."

"Despot," she laughed back as he patted her hand at the door, "if you only had a kind heart I should love you—a little!"

On the way home to her tiny apartment in the Rue de Grenelle, where she lived with her aunt and her younger sister, who was a student of drawing, she walked through the Garden of the Luxembourg, thinking about a concert. Not one of those which the master had forbidden to her, but a very simple and foolish and far-away little concert in the old hotel beside the Delaware. And the deep beauty of the forest came back to her, and the long-shining reaches of the river, and the hours of good comradeship with a boy who perfectly shared her joy of living, and the breath of the pine-trees and the sweetness of the wild grape! Did she really smell them now? No, it was only the faint fragrance of the formal beds of hyacinths and tulips and jonquils on the terraces behind the old palace. In the broad walks, children were running and playing. Old men were smoking on the benches in a drowsy peace. In the shady paths under the tall trees, evidently amatory couples were strolling or sitting close together. Carola enjoyed it all—but there was a look in her face, half sad, half smiling, as if she remembered something better.

When she reached home, she laid aside her hat and scarf, and went into the little *salon*. She sat down at the piano and let her fingers run idly over the keys, wandering from fragment to fragment of soft music. Then with a firmer touch she began to play the *humoreske* of Dvořák, but with a new phrasing, a new expression. It was full of an infinite tenderness, a great longing, a sweetness of distant and remembered joy. It seemed to be singing over again the favourite song of some one who had died—singing very clearly and distinctly so as not to lose a single note, a single movement, of the unforgotten melody of happiness.

The delicate dusk of a May evening gathered slowly in the room. The windows were wide open. In the narrow, curving street below, already half-deserted, a young man who was passing with long aimless steps, as if he felt that he must be going somewhere but did not know exactly where, stopped suddenly when he heard the music above him, and stood listening until its last note trembled into silence. Then he strode away, but in the opposite direction, as if he had changed his mind.

II

The path that had led Richard Shafer into the Rue de Grenelle and under the windows of Carola Brune without knowing it, was long and roundabout, and in places rather rough. It was one of the by-ways of the unknown quantity.

To him, from the first, the thought of the perfect summer had been like something that he had lost and would never find again. It made him dissatisfied, fickle, and resentful. He went back to his college work with a temper which handicapped him in everything. His lessons seemed like the dullest drudgery to one who felt sure that he had in him the making of a poet or a musician, he did not quite know which—perhaps it was both. The fellowship of the other boys, with its rude and hearty democracy, streaked with funny little social prejudices and ambitions, was a thing of which he could not or would not learn the secret.

He tried running with the literary set. But Shorty Burke, who was the acknowledged college genius, said of him, "Shafer seems to think that he's the only man since Keats, and all the rest of us are duffers."

He tried running with the fast set. But Duke Jones, who could carry more strong liquors than any man in the crowd, said of him, "Dick is no good; when he goes to town with us he's a thousand miles away, and every glass makes him more stuck-up and quarrelsome."

He tried running with the purely social set, the arbiters of college elegance. But it bored him immensely, and he took no pains to conceal it, so they silently cast him out.

The consequence of all this was that he failed to get into any of the upper-class societies, and consoled himself with the belief that he was terribly in love with a girl three years older than himself.

She was part of a liberal education, and she was very kind to him because she liked his really beautiful violin playing. When she told him, at the beginning of his senior year, that she was going to marry one of the assistant professors, he added another illustration to his theory that "all girls are like that," and plunged into a violent course of study for honours and a fellowship. But it was too late. He graduated with a fourth group and a firm conviction that college is a failure.

Then he went to New York, with his violin and with a dozen poems and half-a-dozen short stories in his trunk, resolved to storm the magazines or to get a place in one of the great orchestras—he was not quite sure which of the two short paths to fame it would be.

It was neither. He sold two sonnets and a story which brought him in $47.50. For a few months he saw life in the Great White Way and other paths, and found them very dusty. It would not be true to say that there was no amusement in it. There were times when it was excessively merry. And for the little *Caffè Fiammella*, where the fat, bald-headed proprietor used to introduce him as "*l'illustrissimo violinista Signore Ricardo Sciafèro*," and where the mixed audience welcomed his music with delight, he had a sincere affection, in spite of the ineradicable smell of garlic. There was a girl there who was the living image of Raphæl's *Fornarina*, until she began to talk.

But in all the life that he thus confusedly saw, there was not a single hour to which he could have said with Faust, "Oh, stay, thou art so fair!" For behind it all, there was that inward, unconscious standard of beauty and happiness—the summer which he could not have forgotten if he would, and would not have forgotten if he could. It did not console or comfort him at all. It only kept him from being contented—which, after all, would have been the worst thing in the world for him at the present stage of his education.

So when the remnant of his patrimony had shrunk to a couple of hundred dollars, he burned his poems and stories, for which he had conceived a strong disgust, and took passage on a small French steam-ship for Bordeaux, to make the "grand tour" of Europe. His violin made him the most popular person on the ship. He had a facile talent and a good memory, which enabled him to play almost any kind of music; and when he could not remember he could improvise. The second officer, a short, stout man, with a pointed black beard, and a secret passion for the fine arts, conceived a great fancy for the young American. When they reached Bordeaux he took Richard to his favourite theatre and introduced him to the leader of the orchestra, a person with a crinkly yellow face and a soft heart, whose name was Camembert, for which reason his intimates called him "the Cheese."

The theatre was about to close for the summer, but four of the musicians had made a plan for a concert tour in various small cities and watering-places. When M. Camembert had heard Richard play after a joyous supper in the famous restaurant of the *Chapon Fin*, he embraced him with effusion and invited him to join the company.

Nothing could have suited the young man's humour better. They wandered from one city-in-etching to another,—Angoulême, Poitiers, Tours, Rennes, Caen,—grey and crumbly towns, white and trim towns. They visited the rocky resorts of Brittany and the sandy resorts of Normandy. They played in a little theatre, or in a casino, or in the ballroom of a hotel. Their fortunes varied, but in the main they were prosperous. The announcements of "The Renowned Camembert Quintette, with a celebrated American Soloist" attracted an amused curiosity. And the music was good, for the old man was a real master, and the practice was strenuous and persistent. It was hard work, but it was also good fun, and the great thing for Richard was that he learned more of the human side of music and of the philosophy of life than he could have done in ten years of insulated study.

A vein of luck which they struck in Rouen and Dieppe emboldened them to turn eastward, with comfortably full pockets, and try the Dauphiné and High Savoy. At Grenoble they had a frost and a heavy loss, but at the sleepy Baths of Uriage they made a week of good harvest with afternoon recitals. Chambréy did well for them, and Annécy even better, so that, in spite of the indifference of Aix, they reached Geneva in funds. Then they played their way around the Lake of Geneva, and up into the Rhone Valley, and so over to the Italian lakes with the autumn.

Here, at Pallanza, in a garden overhanging the Lago Maggiore where the Borromean Isles sleep in their swan-like beauty on the blue-green waves, they faced the question of turning homeward or going on to the south for a winter tour. As they sat around the little iron table, which held a savoury Spanish omelette and a corpulent straw-covered flask of Chianti, their spirit was cheerful and their courage high.

"Why not?" asked the valiant Camembert. "Is it that the Italians are more difficult to conquer than the French? Napoleon did it—my faith, yes. Forward to the conquest of Italy!"

Richard was immensely amused. He did not really care which way they went, as long as they went somewhere. His heart was full of a vague hunger for home,—deep, wild, sheltering woods, friendly hills, companionable and never-failing little rivers,—he longed to be there. But he knew that was impossible. So why not Italy? It would certainly be an adventure.

And so it was. But the conquest was largely a matter of imagination. They saw the flowing green streets of Venice, the ruddy towers of Bologna, the grey walls and dark dome of Florence. They saw the fountains flash in Rome and the red fire run down the long slope of Vesuvius at Naples. They crossed over to Sicily and saw ivory Palermo in her golden shell and Taormina sitting high upon the benches of her amphitheatre. In that sense they conquered and possessed Italy, as any one who has eyes and a heart may do.

But Italy did not pay much tribute to their music. They had to travel third-class and sleep in the poorest inns, cultivating a taste for macaroni and dark bread with pallid butter. Still, they were merry enough until they reached Genoa, and perceived that there was no reasonable prospect of their being able to make anything at all in the over-civilised and over-entertained towns of the Rivièra.

"We must retreat, my children," said the Cheese, crinkling his face over the sour wine in a musty *trattoria*, "but let us retreat in good order and while we have the means to do so. How much money in bank?"

They counted their resources and found them hardly enough to pay the railway fare to Bordeaux. Richard insisted upon putting the remnant of his private fortune into the common fund, but the others would not have it.

"No," they said, "you shall not give us money. But you may settle all the restaurant bills between here and Bordeaux."

"But I am not going to Bordeaux," said he; "I am going to Paris."

At this there was voluble protest and discussion. Richard had no arguments, but his determination was as fixed as it was unreasonable. Finally he forced them to take fifty francs as a loan. At Lyons the quintette dissolved with emotional embraces, the four going westward, and he northward in the night train.

When he walked out into the stony desert in front of the *Gare de Lyon* in the grey chill of a March morning, he had just two hundred and twenty francs in his pocket, and he felt that he was really adrift in the world. There was nothing for him to hold fast to, no one who had need of him.

He found a garret room in the *Rue Cherche Midi*, and looked up two friends of his who were studying at the *Beaux Arts*. They introduced him to a newspaper correspondent who threw a bit of work in his way—a fortnightly letter to an Arkansas paper on French fashions and society, at five dollars *per* letter. This did not go very far, but it retarded the melting away of his estate while he finished two articles,—one on "The Cradle of the French Revolution," the Chateau of Vezille, which he had visited during his week at the Baths of Uriage,—the other on "An Eruption of Vesuvius," which had opportunely occurred while he was in Naples. For the first time in his life he wrote directly, simply, and naturally, describing what he had really seen, and expressing what he had really felt and imagined. He sent the articles to two American magazines and relapsed into a state of doubt and despair.

He took what Paris has to give a young man in the way of cheap diversion, but he found it as dusty as New York. The long rambles through the older parts of the city, the solitary excursions into the forests of the environs, really satisfied and refreshed him more. Meantime the feeling that he was adrift grew upon him and his reserve of capital disappeared. The wolf scratched at the door of his garret and short rations were necessary. In the second week of May a remittance arrived from the Arkansas paper for his last two letters, with the statement that they were not "snappy" enough to suit the taste of the community, and that the correspondence had better be discontinued.

So it was that he strode through the Rue de Grenelle in the May twilight, with fifty francs in his pocket, resolved to spend it all that night—and then? Well, it was not very clear in his mind, but certainly he was not going back to his miserable lodging,—and surely there must be some way of making an end of it all for a man who felt that he was adrift and very tired,—there was no one to care much if he dropped out, and he could see no attractive reason for going on.

It was then that he heard the notes of the *humoreske* coming down into the deserted street and stood still to listen. The memories of the perfect summer floated around him again. Something in the music seemed to call to him, to plead with him, to try to console and cheer him with a wonderful, playful tenderness like the pure wordless sympathy of a child.

"If she had only known how to play it like that," he said to himself; "if she had only cared enough—she would have called me back. But here is a woman who does know—and perhaps even for me—well, I will fight a little longer."

So he turned back to his lonely lodging, guided and impelled by something that he could not quite understand, and did not even try to explain. Surely it would be absurd to think that the chance hearing of a bit of music could have an influence on a man's life.

III

That turn in the Rue de Grenelle seemed like the turn in the tide of his fortunes. The morning mail brought an order for five hundred francs, with a letter from the editor of the *Epoch Magazine*, saying that he liked the article on "The Cradle of the Revolution" very much, and that he wished the author would do three papers for him on the "Old Prisons of Paris," A week later came a letter from the editor of *The World's Wonders*, saying that if the author of the excellent article on Vesuvius would procure photographic illustrations of it at their expense, they would be glad to pay a hundred dollars for it, and asking if he felt like doing two or three articles on "The Little Chateaux of France" during the summer.

Richard felt, not so much that he was "himself again," but that he was a new man. The touch of praise for his work refreshed him more than wine. His friends, the *Beaux Arts* men and the newspaper correspondent, noticed the change in him, and accused him of being in love.

"Not much," he laughed, "but I am at work—two articles accepted and commissions for five more."

They joyfully gave him all the hints and helps they could, and told him where to find the books that he needed. He settled down to his reading bravely and made copious notes for his articles. On Sundays he went with his three friends to spend the day at some resort in the suburbs. He played the violin only on these country excursions and at night in his room when his eyes were tired. The rest of the time he toiled terribly. His boyish dream that the world lay at his feet was ended, but instead he felt that he had the power to do something fairly good, if he worked hard enough. And then, perhaps some day he might have the good luck to meet that girl whose music he had heard the evening when the tide turned.

He wondered what she looked like. He had passed the house often, hoping that he might see her or hear her play again. But nothing of that kind happened. The windows on the second floor were always closed. A discreet inquiry at the glass door of the *concierge* drew out only the information that Madame Farr, the American lady, had gone away with her two nieces for their vacation. The name conveyed nothing to him. It would have been absurd to try to follow such a cobweb clue, and give up his work to chase after an unknown American lady and her invisible nieces.

Yet more and more the remembrance of that strain of music lingered with him, strangely penetrating and significant. He played it often on the violin. It came to be the symbol of that summer, not as it had ended in disappointment and deception, but as it had flowed for so many perfect weeks in pure joy and gaiety of heart. He thought of the unseen player very kindly. He tried unconsciously to make a picture of her in his mind—the colour of her hair, her eyes, the shape of her face. He saw her running through the woods, or sitting between the knees of the old hemlock beside the river. And always her hair was blond and soft and loosely curling, her eyes of a brown so bright and clear that it seemed to glow with hidden gold, and her face a full oval, tinted like the petal of a great magnolia blossom.

"I am a poor fool," he would say to himself after these reveries; "why should she have been in the least like Carola? More probably she had freckles and red hair—but she was a girl who understood."

When August came, Richard's friends went off for a holiday, but he stuck to his work. The heat of Paris was faint and smothering. On the first Sunday he went out to St. Germain, loveliest of all the Parisian suburbs, and wandered all day in the green and mossy forest. He was lonely and depressed. Not even the cool verdure of the woods, nor the splendour of the view from the terrace looking out over the curves of the Seine, and the green rolling hills, and the lines of light that led to the city beginning to glow with a pale yellow radiance in the dusk, could console him. The merry, companionable stir of life around him made him feel more solitary. He turned away from the gay verandah of the *Pavillion Henry IV*, which was full of dining-parties, and went back into the town to seek the quieter garden of the *Pavillion Louis XIV*. There was a big linden-tree there and a certain table at one side of it where he had dined before. He would go there now for his solitary repast.

But the garden also was well-patronized that night. The white-aproned waiters were running to and fro; the stout landlady in black silk and a lace cap was moving among her guests with beaming face; a soft babble of talk and laughter rose from every walk and corner. When Richard came to his chosen table he found it occupied by three ladies. Disappointed, he was turning to look for another place, when the voice of Carola Brune called him.

When a thing like that happens, a man does not know exactly where he is, or how he feels. The largeness and the smallness of the world amaze him; the mystery of life bewilders him; he is confused in the presence of the unknown quantity. How he behaves, what he says or does, depends entirely upon instincts beyond his control.

Richard would have been puzzled to give an account of his introduction to Mrs. Farr, and of his recognition of the little sister, now grown to young womanhood. The conversation at the table where he dined with the family party was very vague in his mind. He knew that he was telling them about his adventures, as if they were scenes in a comedy, and that he said a little about the turn of good luck that had come to him just in time. He knew that Carola was talking of her music-lessons, and of her dear master and of his sudden promise that she should have a concert in the early winter. It was all very jolly and friendly, but it did not seem quite real to him until he asked her a question.

"Where did you live in Paris last May?"

"In the Rue de Grenelle," she answered; "of course you know that old street."

He nodded and fell into silence, letting his cigarette go out, as he sipped his coffee.

"Well," he said, "this has been delightful—it was great luck to meet you. But I suppose I should be going. The best of friends must part."

"But no," said Carola, flushing faintly, "what reason is there for that stupid proverb now? My aunt and sister always take a little walk on the terrace after dinner to see the lights. But you must let me show you what pretty rooms we have found here for our vacation. I have to be near the master and to keep up my practising, you know. I have a heavenly piano. Don't you want to hear whether I have improved in my playing?"

"I do," he answered, "indeed that is just what I want."

When they came into the little sitting-room above the garden, the windows were wide and the room was cool and dim and fragrant. Carola moved about in the shadow, lighting the candles on the mantle-piece and the tall lamp beside the piano.

"Now," she said, "let us talk a little."

He hesitated a moment, and answered: "I would rather hear you play."

"You are as decided and dictatorial as ever," she laughed; "but this time you shall have your way. What will you have—a bit of Chopin or Grieg? Here is plenty of music to choose from."

"No," he said, "something that you know by heart. The piece that you played in the Rue de Grenelle in the twilight on May the seventh."

She looked at him with startled, wondering eyes, as if about to ask the explanation of such a curious request. Then her eyes dropped, and her colour rose, and she sat down at the piano.

The *humoreske* came from her lightly moving hands as it had come on that spring evening,—quaint, tender, consoling, caressing,—but now with a new accent of joy in it, a quicker, almost exulting movement in the dancing passages. Richard listened, standing close behind her, watching the play of her firm, rounded fingers, breathing the fragrance that rose from her hair and her white neck.

When she turned on the stool he was kneeling beside her, and his hands were stretched out to take hers.

"Let me tell you," he exclaimed, "let me tell you what a fool I have been."

So she sat very still while he told her of his failure at college, and how he had gone wild afterward, and how bitter he had been, and how lonely. The adventure with the travelling musicians had led to nothing, and his assurance of winning fame with his violin or with his pen had come to nothing. He was at the edge of the big darkness on that May evening, when she had brought the turn of the tide without knowing it. And even now things were not much better, but still he had a fighting chance to make himself amount to something. He could write, and he would work at it as a man must work at his calling. He could play the violin, and he would make it his avocation and refreshment. She was going on, he knew, to win a great success. He would rejoice in it—he loved her with all his heart—she must know that—but he had nothing to offer her. He was too poor to ask her for anything now.

Her hands trembled as he bent to kiss them. In her shining eyes there was a strange, sweet, deep smile. She leaned over him, and he felt the warmth of her breath on his forehead as she whispered: "Richard, couldn't you even ask me for the *humoreske*?"

HALF-TOLD TALES: AN OLD GAME

Three men were taking a walk together, as they said, just to while away the time.

The first man intended to go Somewhere, to look at a piece of property which he was considering. The second man was ready to go Anywhere, since he expected to be happy by the way. The third man thought he was going Nowhere, because he was a philosopher and held that time and space are only mental forms.

Therefore the third man walked in silence, reflecting upon the vanity of whiling away an hour which did not exist, and upon the futility of going when staying was the same thing. But the other men, being more simple, were playing the oldest game in the world and giving names to the things that they saw as they travelled.

"Mutton," said the Somewhere Man, as he looked over a stone wall.

"A flock of sheep," said the Anywhere Man, gazing upon the pasture, where the fleecy ewes were nipping grass between the rocks and the eager lambs nuzzled their mothers.

But the Nowhere Man meditated on the foolish habit of eating, and said nothing.

"An ant-hill," said the Anywhere Man, looking at a mound beside the path; "see how busy the citizens are!"

"Pismires," said the Somewhere Man, kicking the mound; "they sting like the devil."

But the Nowhere Man, being certain that the devil is a myth, said nothing.

"Briars," said the Somewhere Man, as they passed through a coppice.

"Blackberries," said the Anywhere Man; "they will blossom next month and ripen in August."

But the Nowhere Man, to whom they referred the settlement of the first round of the game, decided that both had lost because they spoke only of accidental phenomena.

With the next round they came into a little forest on a sandy hill. The oak-trees were still bare, and the fir-trees were rusty green, and the maple-trees were in rosy bud. On these things the travellers were agreed.

But among the withered foliage on the ground a vine trailed far and wide with verdant leaves, thick and heavy, and under the leaves were clusters of rosy stars, breathing a wonderful sweetness, so that the travellers could not but smell it.

"Rough-leaf," said the Somewhere Man; "gravel-weed we call it in our country, because it marks the poorest soil."

"Trailing arbutus," said the Anywhere Man; "May-flowers we call them in our country."

"But why?" asked the Nowhere Man. "May has not yet come."

“She is coming,” answered the other; “she will be here before these are gone.”

On the other side of the wood they entered a meadow where a little bird was bubbling over with music in the air.

“Skunk-blackbird,” said the Somewhere Man; “colours the same as a skunk.”

“Bobolink,” said the Anywhere Man; “spills his song while he flies.”

“It is a silly name,” said the Nowhere Man. “Where did you find it?”

“I don’t know,” answered the other; “it just sounds to me like the bird.”

By this time it was clear that the two men did not play the game by the same rules, but they went on playing, just as other people do.

They saw a little thatched house beside the brook. “Beastly hovel,” said the first man. “Pretty cottage,” said the second.

A woman was tossing and fondling her child, with kiss-words. “Sickly sentiment,” said the first man. “Mother love,” said the second.

They passed a youth sleeping on the grass under a tree. “Lazy hound!” said the first man. “Happy dog!” said the second.

Now the third man, remembering that he was a philosopher, concluded that he was wasting his imaginary time in hearing this endless old game.

“I must bid you good-day, gentlemen,” said he, “for it seems to me that you are disputing only about appearances, and are not likely to arrive Somewhere or Anywhere. But I am seeking *das Ding an sich.*[1]”

So he left them, and went on his way Nowhere. And I know not which of the others won the game, but I think the second man had more pleasure in playing it.

1 ‘The thing in itself.’ Reference to Kant’s philosophy about an object as it is, without ‘meaning’ applied.

HALF-TOLD TALES: THE UNRULY SPRITE

A PARTIAL FAIRY TALE

There was once a man who was also a writer of books.

The merit of his books lies beyond the horizon of this tale. No doubt some of them were good, and some of them were bad, and some were merely popular. But he was all the time trying to make them better, for he was quite an honest man, and thankful that the world should give him a living for his writing. Moreover, he found great delight in the doing of it, which was something that did not enter into the world's account—a kind of daily Christmas present in addition to his wages.

But the interesting thing about the man was that he had a clan or train of little sprites attending him—small, delicate, aerial creatures, who came and went around him at their pleasure, and showed him wonderful things, and sang to him, and kept him from being discouraged, and often helped him with his work.

If you ask me what they were and where they came from, I must frankly tell you that I do not know. Neither did the man know. Neither does anybody else know.

But the man had sense enough to understand that they were real—just as real as any of the other mysterious things, like microbes, and polonium, and chemical affinities, and the northern lights, by which we are surrounded. Sometimes it seemed as if the sprites were the children of the flowers that die in blooming; and sometimes as if they came in a flock with the birds from the south; and sometimes as if they rose one by one from the roots of the trees in the deep forest, or from the waves of the sea when the moon lay upon them; and sometimes as if they appeared suddenly in the streets of the city after the people had passed by and the houses had gone to sleep. They were as light as thistle-down, as unsubstantial as mists upon the mountain, as wayward and flickering as will-o'-the-wisps. But there was something immortal about them, and the man knew that the world would be nothing to him without their presence and comradeship.

Most of these attendant sprites were gentle and docile; but there was one who had a strain of wildness in him. In his hand he carried a bow, and at his shoulder a quiver of arrows, and he looked as if, some day or other, he might be up to mischief.

Now this man was much befriended by a certain lady, to whom he used to bring his stories in order that she might tell him whether they were good, or bad, or merely popular. But whatever she might think of the stories, always she liked the man, and of the airy fluttering sprites she grew so fond that it almost seemed as if they were her own children.

This was not unnatural, for they were devoted to her; they turned the pages of her book when she read; they made her walks through the forest pleasant and friendly; they lit lanterns for her in the dark; they brought flowers to her and sang to her, as well as to the man. Of this he was glad, because of his great friendship for the lady and his desire to see her happy.

But one day she complained to him of the sprite who carried the bow. "He is behaving badly," said she; "he teases me."

"That surprises me," said the man, "and I am distressed to hear it; for at heart he is rather good, and to you he is deeply attached. But how does he tease you, dear lady? What does he do?"

"Oh, nothing," she answered, "and that is what annoys me. The others are all busy with your affairs or mine. But this idle one follows me like my shadow, and looks at me all the time. It is not at all polite. I fear he has a vacant mind and has not been well brought up."

"That may easily be," said the man, "for he came to me very suddenly one day, and I have never inquired about his education."

"But you ought to do so," said she; "it is your duty to have him taught to know his place, and not to tease, and other useful lessons."

"You are always right," said the man, "and it shall be just as you say."

On the way home he talked seriously to the sprite, and told him how impolite he had been, and arranged a plan for his schooling in botany, diplomacy, music, psychology, deportment, and other useful studies.

The rest of the sprites came in to the school-room every day, to get some of the profitable lessons. They sat around quiet and orderly, so that it was quite like a kindergarten. But the principal pupil was restless and troublesome.

"You are never still," said the man; "you have an idle mind and wandering thoughts."

"No!" said the sprite, shaking his head. "It is true, my mind is not on my lessons. But my thoughts do not wander at all. They always follow yours."

Then the man stopped talking, and the other sprites laughed behind their hands. But the one who had been reproved went on drawing pictures in the back of his botany book. The face in the pictures was always the same, but none of them seemed to satisfy him, for he always rubbed them out and began over again.

After several weeks of hard work the master thought his pupil must have learned something, so he gave him a holiday, and asked him what he would like to do.

"Go with you," he answered, "when you take her your new stories."

So they went together, and the lady complimented the writer on his success as an educator.

"Your pupil does you credit," said she; "he talks very nicely about botany and deportment. But I am a little troubled to see him looking so pale. Perhaps you have been too severe with him. I must take him out in the garden with me every day to play a while."

"You have a kind heart," said the man, "and I hope he will appreciate it."

This agreeable and amicable life continued for some weeks, and everybody was glad that affairs had arranged themselves. But one day the lady brought a new complaint.

"He is a strange little creature, and he has begun to annoy me in the most extraordinary way."

"That is bad," said the man. "What does he do now?"

"Oh, nothing," she answered, "and that is just the trouble. When I want to talk about you, he refuses, and says he does not like you as much as he used to. When I propose to play a game, he says he is tired and would rather sit under a tree and hear stories. When I tell them he says they do not suit him, they all end happily, and that is stupid. He is very perverse. But he clings to me like a bur. He is always teasing me to tell him the name of every flower in my garden and give him one of every kind."

"Is he rude about it?"

"Not exactly rude, but he is all the more annoying because he is so polite, and I always feel that he wants something different."

"He must not do that," said the man. "He must learn to want what you wish."

"But how can he learn what I wish? I do not always know that myself."

"It may be difficult," said the man, "but all the same he must learn it for your sake. I will deal with him."

So he took the unruly sprite out into the desert and gave him a sound beating with thorn branches. The blood ran down the poor little creature's arms and legs, and the tears down the man's cheeks. But the only words that he said were: "You must learn to want what she wishes—do you hear?—you must want what she wishes." At last the sprite whimpered and said: "Yes, I hear; I will wish what she wants." Then the man stopped beating him, and went back to his house, and wrote a little story that was really good.

But the sprite lay on his face in the desert for a long time, sobbing as if his heart would break. Then he fell asleep and laughed in his dreams. When he awoke it was night and the moon was shining silver. He rubbed his eyes and whispered to himself: "Now I must find out what she wants." With that he leaped up, and the moonbeams washed him white as he passed through them to the lady's house.

The next afternoon, when the man came to read her the really good story, she would not listen.

"No," she said, "I am very angry with you."

"Why?"

"You know well enough."

"Upon my honour, I do not."

"What?" cried the lady. "You profess ignorance, when he distinctly said——"

"Pardon," said the man; "but *who* said?"

"Your unruly sprite," she answered, indignant. "He came last night outside my window, which was wide open for the moon, and shot an arrow into my breast—a little baby arrow, but it hurt. And when I cried out for the pain, he climbed up to me and kissed the place, saying that would make it well. And he swore that you made him promise to come. If that is true, I will never speak to you again."

"Then of course," said the man, "it is not true. And now what do you want me to do with this unruly sprite?"

"Get rid of him," said she firmly.

"I will," replied the man, and he bowed over her hand and went away.

He stayed for a long time—nearly a week—and when he came back he brought several sad verses with him to read. "They are very dull," said the lady; "what is the matter with you?" He confessed that he did not know, and began to talk learnedly about the Greek and Persian poets, until the lady was consumed with a fever of dullness.

"You are simply impossible!" she cried. "I wonder at myself for having chosen such a friend!"

"I am sorry indeed," said the man.

"For what?"

"For having disappointed you as a friend, and also for having lost my dear unruly sprite who kept me from being dull."

"Lost him!" exclaimed the lady. "How?"

"By now," said the man, "he must be quite dead, for I tied him to a tree in the forest five days ago and left him to starve."

"You are a brute," said the lady, "and a very stupid man. Come, take me to the tree. At least we can bury the poor sprite, and then we shall part forever."

So he took her by the hand and guided her through the woods, and they talked much of the sadness of parting forever.

When they came to the tree, there was the little sprite, with his wrists and ankles bound, lying upon the moss. His eyes were closed, and his body was white as a snowdrop. They knelt down, one on each side of him, and untied the cord. To their surprise his hands felt warm. "I believe he is not quite dead," said the lady. "Shall we try to bring him to life?" asked the man. And with that they fell to chafing his wrists and his palms. Presently he gave each of them a slight pressure of the fingers.

"Did you feel that?" cried she.

"Indeed I did," the man answered. "It shook me to the core. Would you like to take him on your lap so that I can chafe his feet?"

The lady nodded and took the soft little body on her knees and held it close to her, while the man kneeled before her rubbing the small, milk-white feet with strong and tender touches. Presently, as they were thus engaged, they heard the sprite faintly whispering, while one of his eyelids flickered:

"I think—if each of you—would kiss me—on opposite cheeks—at the same moment—those kind of movements would revive me."

The two friends looked at each other, and the man spoke first.

"He talks ungrammatically, and I think he is an incorrigible little savage, but I love him. Shall we try his idea?"

"If you love him," said the lady, "I am willing to try, provided you shut your eyes."

So they both shut their eyes and tried.

But just at that moment the unruly sprite slipped down, and put his hands behind their heads, and the two mouths that sought his cheeks met lip to lip in a kiss so warm, so long, so sweet that everything else was forgotten.

Now you can easily see that as the persons who had this strange experience were the ones who told me the tale, their forgetfulness at this point leaves it of necessity half-told. But I know from other sources that the man who was also a writer went on making books, and the lady always told him truly whether they were good, or bad, or merely popular. But what the unruly sprite is doing now nobody knows.

HALF-TOLD TALES: A CHANGE OF AIR

There were three neighbours who lived side by side in a certain village. They were bound together by the contiguousness of their back yards and front porches, and by a community of interest in taxes and water-rates and the high cost of living. They were separated by their religious opinions; for one of them was a Mystic, and the second was a Sceptic, and the other was a suppressed Dyspeptic who called himself an Asthmatic.

These differences were very dear to them, and laid the foundations of a lasting friendship in a nervous habit of interminable argument on all possible subjects. Their wives did not share in these disputations because they were resolved to be neighbourly, and they could not conceive a difference of opinion without a personal application. So they called one another Clara and Caroline and Katharine, and kissed audibly whenever they met, but they were careful to confine their conversation to topics upon which they had only one mind, such as the ingratitude of domestic servants.

The husbands, however, as often as they could get together without the mollifying influence of the feminine presence, continued their debates with delightful ferocity, finding matter in each event of life, though clear, and especially in those which had not yet occurred. So they had a very happy time, and their friendship deepened from day to day.

"I can see your point of view," one of them would say, after an apparently harmless proposition had been advanced. "Perhaps so," the other would reply, clinging desperately to the advantage of the first service in definitions, "but you certainly do not understand it."

Whereupon the third had the pleasure of showing that neither of the others knew what he was talking about. This invariably resulted in their combining against him, and usually to his gain, because he was able to profit by the inconsistencies of their double play.

But of all earthly pleasures, as Sancho Panza said, there cometh in the end satiety. The neighbours, after several years of refreshing colloquial combat, felt an alarming decline of virility and the approach of an anæmic peace. Their arguments grew monotonous, remote, repetitious, amounting to little more than a bald statement of position: "Here I stand"—"There you stand"—"There he stands,"—"What is the use of talking about it?" The salt and pepper had vanished from their table of conversation, and as each man silently chewed his own favourite cereal, they all felt as if the banqueting-days were ended and each must say to the others:

"Grow old apart from me,
The worst is yet to be."

One night as they were about to separate, long before midnight, without a single spirited controversy, they looked at one another sadly, as men who felt the approach of a common misfortune.

"The trouble is," said the Mystic, who disliked nothing so much as solitude, "we do not meditate enough, and so the springs of our inspiration from the Oversoul are running dry."

"The trouble is," said the Sceptic, whose doubts were more dogmatic than dogmas, "that our fixed ideas are choking the feed-pipes of our minds."

"The trouble is," wheezed the Asthmatic, whose suppressed dyspepsia gave him an enormous appetite, "modern life is demoralised, especially in domestic service. In the last month my wife has had five cooks, and she whom she now has is not a cook. Hygiene is the basis of sound thinking."

This sudden and unexpected renewal of the joy of disputation cheered them greatly, and they discussed it for several hours, arriving, as usual, at the same practical conclusions from the most diverse premises.

They all agreed that the trouble *was*.

To cure it nothing could be better than a change of air. So they resolved to make a little journey together.

They went first to New York, and the size of it impressed them immensely. The Sceptic was delighted with the Cathedral of St. John the Divine, because, as he said, it was so unmistakably human. The Mystic was delighted with the theatres, because, as he said, most of the plays seemed so super-human. The Asthmatic was delighted with the subway, because, as he said, the ventilation was so satisfactory. It was like eating bread-pudding on a steam-boat; you knew exactly what you were getting; all the microbes were blended, and they neutralised each other.

Their next point of visitation was Chicago, where they had heard that a new Literary School was arising with a noise like thunder out of the lake. They attended many club-meetings, and revolved rapidly in the highest literary circles, coming around invariably to the point from which they had started.

"This is tiresome," said the Mystic; "the Oversoul is not in it."

"It is narrowing," said the Sceptic; "these people are the most bigoted unbelievers I ever saw."

"It is unwholesome," said the Asthmatic, "but I think I could digest the stuff if I could only breathe more easily. This wind is too strong for me."

So they agreed to go to Philadelphia for a rest. The clerk in the colonial hotel to which they repaired assured them that the house was crowded—he had only one room, a parlour, which he could fit up with three beds if they would accept it.

The room was large and old-fashioned. A tall bookcase with glass doors stood against the wall. The three beds were arranged, side by side, in the middle of the room. "This is like home," cried the neighbours, and they lay until midnight in a sweet ferocity of dispute over the moral character of Benjamin Franklin.

A couple of hours later the Asthmatic was awakened from a sound sleep by a terrible attack of short breathing.

"Open the window," he gasped; "I am choking to death."

The Mystic sprang from bed and groped along the wall for the electric-light button, but could not find it. Then he groped for the window and his hand touched the glass.

"It is fastened," he cried; "I can't find the catch. It will not move up or down."

"I shall die," groaned the Asthmatic, "unless I have air. Break the window-pane!"

So the Mystic felt for the footstool, over which he had just stubbed his toes, and used the corner of it to smash the glass.

"Ah," said the Asthmatic, with a long sigh of relief, "I am better. There is nothing like fresh air."

Then they all went to sleep again.

The morning roused them slowly, and they lay on their backs looking around the room. The windows were closed and the shades drawn.

But the glass door of the bookcase had a great hole in it!

"You see!" said the Mystic. "It was the faith cure. The Oversoul cured you."

"Not at all," said the Sceptic. "It was the doubt cure. The way to get rid of a thing is to doubt it."

"I think," said the Asthmatic, "that it was the nightmare, and that miscellaneous cooking is the cause of human misery. We have travelled enough, and yet we have found no better air than we left at home."

So they went back to the certain village and continued their disputations very happily for the rest of their lives.

THE NIGHT CALL

I

The first caprice of November snow had sketched the world in white for an hour in the morning. After mid-day, the sun came out, the wind turned warm, and the whiteness vanished from the landscape. By evening, the low ridges and the long plain of New Jersey were rich and sad again, in russet and dull crimson and old gold; for the foliage still clung to the oaks and elms and birches, and the dying monarchy of autumn retreated slowly before winter's cold republic.

In the old town of Calvinton, stretched along the highroad, the lamps were lit early as the saffron sunset faded into humid night. A mist rose from the long, wet street and the sodden lawns, muffling the houses and the trees and the college towers with a double veil, under which a pallid aureole encircled every light, while the moon above, languid and tearful, waded slowly through the mounting fog. It was a night of delay and expectation, a night of remembrance and mystery, lonely and dim and full of strange, dull sounds.

In one of the smaller houses on the main street the light in the window burned late. Leroy Carmichael was alone in his office reading Balzac's story of "The Country Doctor." He was not a gloomy or despondent person, but the spirit of the night had entered into him. He had yielded himself, as young men of ardent temperament often do, to the subduing magic of the fall. In his mind, as in the air, there was a soft, clinging mist, and blurred lights of thought, and a still foreboding of change. A sense of the vast tranquil movement of Nature, of her sympathy and of her indifference, sank deeply into his heart. For a time he realised that all things, and he, too, some day, must grow old; and he felt the universal pathos of it more sensitively, perhaps, than he would ever feel it again.

If you had told Carmichael that this was what he was thinking about as he sat in his bachelor quarters on that November night, he would have stared at you and then laughed.

"Nonsense," he would have answered, cheerfully. "I'm no sentimentalist: only a bit tired by a hard afternoon's work and a rough ride home. Then, Balzac always depresses me a little. The next time I'll take some quinine and Dumas: he is a tonic."

But, in fact, no one came in to interrupt his musings and rouse him to that air of cheerfulness with which he always faced the world, and to which, indeed (though he did not know it), he owed some measure of his delay in winning the confidence of Calvinton.

He had come there some five years ago with a particularly good outfit to practice medicine in that quaint and alluring old burgh, full of antique hand-made furniture and traditions. He had not only been well trained for his profession in the best medical school and hospital of New York, but he was also a graduate of Calvinton College (in which his father had been a professor for a time), and his granduncle was a Grubb, a name high in the Golden Book of Calvintonian aristocracy and inscribed upon tombstones in every village within a radius of fifteen miles. Consequently the young doctor arrived well accredited, and was received in his first year with many tokens of hospitality in the shape of tea-parties and suppers.

But the final and esoteric approval of Calvinton was a thing apart from these mere fashionable courtesies and worldly amenities—a thing not to be bestowed without due consideration and satisfactory reasons. Leroy Carmichael failed, somehow or other, to come up to the requirements for a leading physician in such a conservative community. In the judgment of Calvinton he was a clever young man; but he lacked poise and gravity. He walked too lightly along the streets, swinging his stick, and greeting his acquaintances blithely, as if he were rather glad to be alive. Now this is a sentiment, if you analyse it, near akin to vanity, and, therefore, to be discountenanced in your neighbour and concealed in yourself. How can a man be glad that he is alive, and frankly show it, without a touch of conceit and a reprehensible forgetfulness of the presence of original sin even in the best families? The manners of a professional man, above all, should at once express and impose humility.

Young Dr. Carmichael, Calvinton said, had been spoiled by his life in New York. It had made him too gay, light-hearted, almost frivolous. It was possible that he might know a good deal about medicine, though doubtless that had been exaggerated; but it was certain that his temperament needed chastening before he could win the kind of confidence that Calvinton had given to the venerable Dr. Coffin, whose face was like a monument, and whose practice rested upon the two pillars of podophyllin and predestination.

So Carmichael still felt, after his five years' work, that he was an outsider; felt it rather more indeed than when he had first come. He had enough practice to keep him in good health and spirits. But his patients were along the side streets and in the smaller houses and out in the country. He was not called, except in a chance emergency, to the big houses with the white pillars. The inner circle had not yet taken him in.

He wondered how long he would have to work and wait for that. He knew that things in Calvinton moved slowly; but he knew also that its silent and subconscious judgments sometimes crystallised with incredible rapidity and hardness. Was it possible that he was already classified in the group that came near but did not enter, an inhabitant but not a real burgher, a half-way citizen and a lifelong new-comer? That would be rough; he would not like growing old in that way.

But perhaps there was no such invisible barrier hemming in his path. Perhaps it was only the naturally slow movement of things that hindered him. Some day the gate would open. He would be called in behind those white pillars into the world of which his father had often told him stories and traditions. There he would prove his skill and his worth. He would make himself useful and trusted by his work. Then he could marry the girl he loved, and win a firm place and a real home in the old town whose strange charm held him so strongly even in the vague sadness of this autumnal night.

He turned again from these musings to his Balzac, and read the wonderful pages in which Benassis tells the story of his consecration to his profession and Captain Genestas confides the little Adrien to his care, and then the beautiful letter in which the boy describes the country doctor's death and burial. The simple pathos of it went home to Carmichael's heart.

"It is a fine life, after all," said he to himself, as he shut the book at midnight and laid down his pipe. "No man has a better chance than a doctor to come close to the real thing. Human nature is his patient, and each case is a symptom. It's worth while to work for the sake of getting nearer to the reality and doing some definite good by the way. I'm glad that this isn't one of those mystical towns where Christian Science and Buddhism and all sorts of vagaries flourish. Calvinton may be difficult, but it's not obscure. And some day I'll feel its pulse and get at the heart of it."

The silence of the little office was snapped by the nervous clamour of the electric bell, shrilling with a night call.

II

Dr. Carmichael turned on the light in the hall, and opened the front door. A tall, dark man of military aspect loomed out of the mist, and, behind him, at the curbstone, the outline of a big motorcar was dimly visible. He held out a visiting-card inscribed "Baron de Mortemer," and spoke slowly and courteously, but with a strong nasal accent and a tone of insistent domination.

"You are the Dr. Carmichael, yes? You speak French—no? It is a pity. There is need of you at once—a patient—it is very pressing. You will come with me, yes?"

"But I do not know you, sir," said the doctor; "you are——"

"The Baron de Mortemer," broke in the stranger, pointing to the card as if it answered all questions. "It is the Baroness who is very suffering—I pray you to come without delay."

"But what is it?" asked the doctor. "What shall I bring with me? My instrument-case?"

The Baron smiled with his lips and frowned with his eyes. "Not at all," he said, "Madame expects not an arrival—it is not so bad as that—but she has had a sudden access of anguish—she has demanded you. I pray you to come at the instant. Bring what pleases you, what you think best, but come!"

The man's manner was not agitated, but it was strangely urgent, overpowering, constraining; his voice was like a pushing hand. Carmichael threw on his coat and hat, hastily picked up his medicine-satchel and a portable electric battery, and followed the Baron to the motor.

The great car started easily and rolled softly purring down the deserted street. The houses were all asleep, and the college buildings dark as empty fortresses. The moon-threaded mist clung closely to the town like a shroud of gauze, not concealing the form beneath, but making its immobility more mysterious. The trees drooped and dripped with moisture, and the leaves seemed ready, almost longing, to fall at a touch. It was one of those nights when the solid things of the world, the houses and the hills and the woods and the very earth itself, grow unreal to the point of vanishing; while the impalpable things, the presences of life and death which travel on the unseen air, the influences of the far-off starry lights, the silent messages and presentiments of darkness, the ebb and flow of vast currents of secret existence all around us, seem so close and vivid that they absorb and overwhelm us with their intense reality.

Through this realm of indistinguishable verity and illusion, strangely imposed upon the familiar, homely street of Calvinton, the machine ran smoothly, faintly humming, as the Frenchman drove it with master-skill—itself a dream of embodied power and speed. Gliding by the last cottages of Town's End where the street became the highroad, the car ran swiftly through the open country for a mile until it came to a broad entrance. The gate was broken from the leaning posts and thrown to one side. Here the machine turned in and laboured up a rough, grass-grown carriage-drive.

Carmichael knew that they were at Castle Gordon, one of the "old places" of Calvinton, which he often passed on his country drives. The house stood well back from the road, on a slight elevation, looking down over the oval field that was once a lawn, and the scattered elms and pines and Norway firs that did their best to preserve the memory of a noble plantation. The building was colonial; heavy stone walls covered with yellow stucco; tall white wooden pillars ranged along a narrow portico; a style which seemed to assert that a Greek temple was good enough for the residence of an American gentleman. But the clean buff and white of the house had long since faded. The stucco had cracked, and, here and there, had fallen from the stones. The paint on the pillars was dingy, peeling in round blisters and narrow strips from the grey wood underneath. The trees were ragged and untended, the grass uncut, the driveway overgrown with weeds and gullied by rains—the whole place looked forsaken. Carmichael had always supposed that it was vacant. But he had not passed that way for nearly a month, and, meantime, it might have been reopened and tenanted.

The Baron drove the car around to the back of the house and stopped there.

"Pardon," said he, "that I bring you not to the door of entrance; but this is the more convenient."

He knocked hurriedly and spoke a few words in French. The key grated in the lock and the door creaked open. A withered, wiry little man, dressed in dark grey, stood holding a lighted candle, which flickered in the draught. His head was nearly bald; his sallow, hairless face might have been of any age from twenty to a hundred years; his eyes between their narrow red lids were glittering and inscrutable as those of a snake. As he bowed and grinned, showing his yellow, broken teeth, Carmichael thought that he had never seen a more evil face or one more clearly marked with the sign of the drug-fiend.

"My chauffeur, Gaspard," said the Baron, "also my valet, my cook, my chambermaid, my man to do all, what you call factotum, is it not? But he speaks not English, so pardon me once more."

He spoke a few words to the man, who shrugged his shoulders and smiled with the same deferential grimace while his unchanging eyes gleamed through their slits. Carmichael caught only the word "Madame" while he was slipping off his overcoat, and understood that they were talking of his patient.

"Come," said the Baron, "he says that it goes better, at least not worse—that is always something. Let us mount at the instant."

The hall was bare, except for a table on which a kitchen lamp was burning, and two chairs with heavy automobile coats and rugs and veils thrown upon them. The stairway was uncarpeted, and the dust lay thick under the banisters. At the door of the back room on the second floor the Baron paused and knocked softly. A low voice answered, and he went in, beckoning the doctor to follow.

III

If Carmichael lived to be a hundred he could never forget that first impression. The room was but partly furnished, yet it gave at once the idea that it was inhabited; it was even, in some strange way, rich and splendid. Candles on the mantelpiece and a silver travelling-lamp on the dressing-table threw a soft light on little articles of luxury, and photographs in jewelled frames, and a couple of well-bound books, and a gilt clock marking the half-hour after midnight. A wood fire burned in the wide chimney-place, and before it a rug was spread. At one side there was a huge mahogany four-post bedstead, and there, propped up by the pillows, lay the noblest-looking woman that Carmichael had ever seen.

She was dressed in some clinging stuff of soft black, with a diamond at her breast, and a deep-red cloak thrown over her feet. She must have been past middle age, for her thick, brown hair was already touched with silver, and one lock of snow-white lay above her forehead. But her face was one of those which time enriches; fearless and tender and high-spirited, a speaking face in which the dark-lashed grey eyes were like words of wonder and the sensitive mouth like a clear song. She looked at the young doctor and held out her hand to him.

"I am glad to see you," she said, in her low, pure voice, "very glad! You are Roger Carmichael's son. Oh, I am glad to see you indeed."

"You are very kind," he answered, "and I am glad also to be of any service to you, though I do not yet know who you are."

The Baron was bending over the fire rearranging the logs on the andirons. He looked up sharply and spoke in his strong nasal tone.

"*Pardon! Madame la Baronne de Mortemer, j'ai l'honneur de vous presenter Monsieur le Docteur Carmichael.*[1]"

The accent on the "doctor" was marked. A slight shadow came upon the lady's face. She answered, quietly:

"Yes, I know. The doctor has come to see me because I was ill. We will talk of that in a moment. But first I want to tell him who I am—and by another name. Dr. Carmichael, did your father ever speak to you of Jean Gordon?"

"Why, yes," he said, after an instant of thought, "it comes back to me now quite clearly. She was the young girl to whom he taught Latin when he first came here as a college instructor. He was very fond of her. There was one of her books in his library—I have it now—a little volume of Horace, with a few translations in verse written on the fly-leaves, and her name on the title-page—Jean Gordon. My father wrote under that, 'My best pupil, who left her lessons unfinished.' He was very fond of the book, and so I kept it when he died."

The lady's eyes grew moist, but the tears did not fall. They trembled in her voice.

"I was that Jean Gordon—a girl of fifteen—your father was the best man I ever knew. You look like him, but he was handsomer than you. Ah, no, I was not his best pupil, but his most wilful and ungrateful one. Did he never tell you of my running away—of the unjust suspicions that fell on him—of his voyage to Europe?"

"Never," answered Carmichael. "He only spoke, as I remember, of your beauty and your brightness, and of the good times that you all had when this old house was in its prime."

"Yes, yes," she said, quickly and with strong feeling, "they were good times, and he was a man of honour. He never took an unfair advantage, never boasted of a woman's favour, never tried to spare himself. He was an American man. I hope you are like him."

The Baron, who had been leaning on the mantel, crossed the room impatiently and stood beside the bed. He spoke in French again, dragging the words in his insistent, masterful voice, as if they were something heavy which he laid upon his wife.

Her grey eyes grew darker, almost black, with enlarging pupils. She raised herself on the pillows as if about to get up. Then she sank back again and said, with an evident effort:

"René, I must beg you not to speak in French again. The doctor does not understand it. We must be more courteous. And now I will tell him about my sudden illness to-night. It was the first time—like a flash of lightning—an ice-cold hand of pain——"

Even as she spoke a swift and dreadful change passed over her face. Her colour vanished in a morbid pallor; a cold sweat lay like death-dew on her forehead; her eyes were fixed on some impending horror; her lips, blue and rigid, were strained with an unspeakable, intolerable anguish. Her left arm stiffened as if it were gripped in a vise of

[1] Excuse me! Madam Baroness de Mortemer, I have the honor to introduce to you Dr. Carmichael.

pain. Her right hand fluttered over her heart, plucking at an unseen weight. It seemed as if an invisible, silent death-wind were quenching the flame of her life. It flickered in an agony of strangulation.

"Be quick," cried the doctor; "lay her head lower on the pillows, loosen her dress, warm her hands."

He had caught up his satchel, and was looking for a little vial. He found it almost empty. But there were four or five drops of the yellowish, oily liquid. He poured them on his handkerchief and held it close to the lady's mouth. She was still breathing regularly though slowly, and as she inhaled the pungent, fruity smell, like the odour of a jargonelle pear, a look of relief flowed over her face, her breathing deepened, her arm and her lips relaxed, the terror faded from her eyes.

He went to his satchel again and took out a bottle of white tablets marked "Nitroglycerin." He gave her one of them, and when he saw her look of peace grow steadier, after a minute, he prepared the electric battery. Softly he passed the sponges charged with their mysterious current over her temples and her neck and down her slender arms and blue-veined wrists, holding them for a while in the palms of her hands, which grew rosy.

In all this the Baron had helped as he could, and watched closely, but without a word. He was certainly not indifferent; neither was he distressed; the expression of his black eyes and heavy, passionless face was that of presence of mind, self-control covering an intense curiosity. Carmichael conceived a vague sentiment of dislike for the man.

When the patient rested easily they stepped outside the room together for a moment.

"It is the *angina*, I suppose," droned the Baron, "hein? That is of great inconvenience. But I think it is the false one, that is much less grave—not truly dangerous, hein?"

"My dear sir," answered Carmichael, "who can tell the difference between a false and a true *angina pectoris*, except by a post-mortem? The symptoms are much alike, the result is sometimes identical, if the paroxysm is severe enough. But in this case I hope that you may be right. Your wife's illness is severe, dangerous, but not necessarily fatal. This attack has passed and may not recur for months or even years."

The lip-smile came back under the Baron's sullen eyes.

"Those are the good news, my dear doctor," said he, slowly. "Then we shall be able to travel soon, perhaps to-morrow or the next day. It is of an extreme importance. This place is insufferable to me. We have engagements in Washington—a gay season."

Carmichael looked at him steadily and spoke with deliberation.

"Baron, you must understand me clearly. This is a serious case. If I had not come in time your wife might be dead now. She cannot possibly be moved for a week, perhaps it may take a month fully to restore her strength. After that she must have a winter of absolute quiet and repose."

The Frenchman's face hardened; his brows drew together in a black line, and he lifted his hand quickly with a gesture of irritation. Then he bowed.

"As you will, doctor! And for the present moment, what is it that I may have the honour to do for your patient?"

"Just now," said the doctor, "she needs a stimulant—a glass of sherry or of brandy, if you have it—and a hot-water bag—you have none? Well, then, a couple of bottles filled with hot water and wrapped in a cloth to put at her feet. Can you get them?"

The Baron bowed again, and went down the stairs. As Carmichael returned to the bedroom he heard the droning, insistent voice below calling "Gaspard, Gaspard!"

The great grey eyes were open as he entered the room, and there was a sense of release from pain and fear in them that was like the deepest kind of pleasure.

"Yes, I am much better," said she; "the attack has passed. Will it come again? No? Not soon, you mean. Well, that is good. You need not tell me what it is—time enough for that to-morrow. But come and sit by me. I want to talk to you. Your first name is——"

"Leroy," he answered. "But you are weak; you must not talk much."

"Only a little," she replied, smiling; "it does me good. Leroy was your mother's name—yes? It is not a Calvinton name. I wonder where your father met her. Perhaps in France when he came to look for me. But he did not find me—no, indeed—I was well hidden then—but he found your mother. You are young enough to be my son. Will you be a friend to me for your father's sake?"

She spoke gently, in a tone of infinite kindness and tender grace, with pauses in which a hundred unspoken recollections and appeals were suggested. The young man was deeply moved. He took her hand in his firm clasp.

"Gladly," he said, "and for your sake too. But now I want you to rest."

"Oh," she answered, "I am resting now. But let me talk a little more. It will not harm me. I have been through so much! Twice married—a great fortune to spend—all that the big world can give. But now I am very tired of the whirl. There is only one thing I want—to stay here in Calvinton. I rebelled against it once; but it draws me back. There is a strange magic in the place. Haven't you felt it? How do you explain it?"

"Yes," he said, "I have felt it surely, but I can't explain it, unless it is a kind of ancient peace that makes you wish to be at home here even while you rebel."

She nodded her head and smiled softly.

"That is it," she said, hesitating for a moment. "But my husband—you see he is a very strong man, and he loves the world, the whirling life—he took a dislike to this place at once. No wonder, with the house in such a state! But I have plenty of money—it will be easy to restore the house. Only, sometimes I think he cares more for the money than—but no matter what I think. He wishes to go on at once—to-morrow, if we can. I hate the thought of it. Is it possible for me to stay? Can you help me?"

"Dear lady," he answered, lifting her hand to his lips, "set your mind at rest. I have already told him that it is impossible for you to go for many days. You can arrange to move to the inn to-morrow, and stay there while you direct the putting of your house in order."

A sound in the hallway announced the return of the Baron and Gaspard with the hot-water bottles and the cognac. The doctor made his patient as comfortable as possible for the night, prepared a sleeping-draught, and gave directions for the use of the tablets in an emergency.

"Good night," he said, bending over her. "I will see you in the morning. You may count upon me."

"I do," she said, with her eyes resting on his; "thank you for all. I shall expect you—*au revoir*."

As they went down the stairs he said to the Baron, "Remember, absolute repose is necessary. With that you are safe enough for to-night. But you may possibly need more of the nitrite of amyl. My vial is empty. I will write the prescription, if you will allow me."

"In the dining-room," said the Baron, taking up the lamp and throwing open the door of the back room on the right. The floor had been hastily swept and the rubbish shoved into the fireplace. The heavy chairs stood along the wall. But two of them were drawn up at the head of the long mahogany table, and dishes and table utensils from a travelling-basket were lying there, as if a late supper had been served.

"You see," said the Baron, drawling, "our banquet-hall! Madame and I have dined in this splendour to-night. Is it possible that you write here?"

His secret irritation, his insolence, his contempt spoke clearly enough in his tone. The remark was almost like an intentional insult. For a second Carmichael hesitated. "No," he thought, "why should I quarrel with him? He is only sullen. He can do no harm."

He pulled a chair to the foot of the table, took out his tablet and his fountain-pen, and wrote the prescription. Tearing off the leaf, he folded it crosswise and left it on the table.

In the hall, as he put on his coat he remembered the paper.

"My prescription," he said, "I must take it to the druggist to-night."

"Permit me," said the Baron, "the room is dark. I will take the paper, and procure the drug as I return from escorting the doctor to his residence."

He went into the dark room, groped about for a moment, and returned, closing the door behind him.

"Come, Monsieur," he said, "your work at the Château Gordon is finished for this night. I shall leave you with yourself—at home, as you say—in a few moments. Gaspard—Gaspard, *fermez la porte à clé*![2]"

The strong nasal voice echoed through the house, and the servant ran lightly down the stairs. His master muttered a few sentences to him, holding up his right hand as he did so, with the five fingers extended, as if to impress something on the man's mind.

"Pardon," he said, turning to Carmichael, "that I speak always French, after the rebuke. But this time it is of necessity. I repeat the instruction for the pilules. One at each hour until eight o'clock—five, not more—it is correct? Come, then, our equipage is always harnessed, always ready, how convenient!"

The two men did not speak as the car rolled through the brumous night. A rising wind was sifting the fog. The moon had set. The loosened leaves came whirling, fluttering, sinking through the darkness like a flight of huge dying moths. Now and then they brushed the faces of the travellers with limp, moist wings.

The red night-lamp in the drug-store was still burning. Carmichael called the other's attention to it.

"You have the prescription?"

"Without doubt!" he answered. "After I have escorted you, I shall procure the drug."

The doctor's front door was lit up as he had left it. The light streamed out rather brightly and illumined the Baron's sullen black eyes and smiling lips as he leaned from the car, lifting his cap.

"A thousand thanks, my dear doctor, you have been excessively kind; yes, truly of an excessive goodness for us. It is a great pleasure—how do you tell it in English?—it is a great pleasure to have met you. *Adieu.*"

"Till to-morrow morning!" said Carmichael, cheerfully, waving his hand.

The Baron stared at him curiously, and lifted his cap again.

"*Adieu!*" droned the insistent voice, and the great car slid into the dark.

---

[2] Lock the door with the key!

IV

The next morning was of crystal. It was after nine when Carmichael drove his electric-phaeton down the leaf-littered street, where the country wagons and the decrepit hacks were already meandering placidly, and out along the highroad, between the still green fields. It seemed to him as if the experience of the past night were “such stuff as dreams are made of.” Yet the impression of what he had seen and heard in that firelit chamber—of the eyes, the voice, the hand of that strangely lovely lady—of her vision of sudden death, her essentially lonely struggle with it, her touching words to him when she came back to life—all this was so vivid and unforgettable that he drove straight to Castle Gordon.

The great house was shut up like a tomb: every door and window was closed, except where half of one of the shutters had broken loose and hung by a single hinge. He drove around to the back. It was the same there. A cobweb was spun across the lower corner of the door and tiny drops of moisture jewelled it. Perhaps it had been made in the early morning. If so, no one had come out of the door since night.

Carmichael knocked, and knocked again. No answer. He called. No reply. Then he drove around to the portico with the tall white pillars and tried the front door. It was locked. He peered through the half-open window into the drawing-room. The glass was crusted with dirt and the room was dark. He was trying to make out the outlines of the huddled furniture when he heard a step behind him. It was the old farmer from the nearest cottage on the road.

“Mornin’, doctor! I seen ye comin’ in, and tho’t ye might want to see the house.”

“Good morning, Scudder! I do, if you’ll let me in. But first tell me about these automobile tracks in the drive.”

The old man gazed at him with a kind of dull surprise as if the question were foolish.

“Why, ye made ’em yerself, comin’ up, didn’t ye?”

“I mean those larger tracks—they were made by a much heavier car than mine.”

“Oh,” said the old man, nodding, “them was made by a big machine that come in here las’ week. You see this house ’s bin shet up ’bout ten years, ever sence ol’ Jedge Gordon died. B’longs to Miss Jean—her that run off with the Eye-talyin. She kinder wants to sell it, and kinder not—ye see—”

“Yes,” interrupted Carmichael, “but about that big machine—when did you say it was here?”

“P’raps four or five days ago; I think it was a We’nsday. Two fellers from Philadelfy—said they wanted to look at the house, tho’t of buyin’ it. So I bro’t ’em in, but when they seen the outside of it they said they didn’t want to look at it no more—too big and too crumbly!”

“And since then no one has been here?”

“Not a soul—leastways nobody that I seen. I don’t s’pose you think o’ buyin’ the house, doc’! It’s too lonely for an office, ain’t it?”

“You’re right, Scudder, much too lonely. But I’d like to look through the old place, if you will take me in.”

The hall, with the two chairs and the table, on which a kitchen lamp with a half-inch of oil in it was standing, gave no sign of recent habitation. Carmichael glanced around him and hurried up the stairway to the bedroom. A tall four-poster stood in one corner, with a coverlet apparently hiding a mattress and some pillows. A dressing-table stood against the wall, and in the middle of the floor there were a few chairs. A half-open closet door showed a pile of yellow linen. The daylight sifted dimly into the room through the cracks of the shutters.

"Scudder," said Carmichael, "I want you to look around carefully and tell me whether you see any signs of any one having been here lately."

The old man stared, and turned his eyes slowly about the room. Then he shook his head.

"Can't say as I do. Looks pretty much as it did when me and my wife brushed it up in October. Ye see it's kinder clean fer an old house—not much dust from the road here. That linen and that bed's bin here sence I c'n remember. Them burnt logs mus' be left over from old Jedge Gordon's time. He died in here. But what's the matter, doc'? Ye think tramps or burglers——"

"No," said Carmichael, "but what would you say if I told you that I was called here last night to see a patient, and that the patient was the Miss Jean Gordon of whom you have just told me?"

"What d'ye mean?" said the old man, gaping. Then he gazed at the doctor pityingly, and shook his head. "I know ye ain't a drinkin' man, doc', so I wouldn't say nothin'. But I guess ye bin dreamin'. Why, las' time Miss Jean writ to me—her name's Mortimer now, and her husband's a kinder Barrin or some sorter furrin noble,—she was in Paris, not mor'n two weeks ago! Said she was dyin' to come back to the ol' place agin, but she wa'n't none too well, and didn't guess she c'd manage it. Ef ye said ye seen her here las' night—why—well, I'd jest think ye'd bin dreamin'. P'raps ye're a little under the weather—bin workin' too hard?"

"I never was better, Scudder, but sometimes curious notions come to me. I wanted to see how you would take this one. Now we'll go downstairs again."

The old man laughed, but doubtfully, as if he was still puzzled by the talk, and they descended the creaking, dusty stairs. Carmichael turned at once into the dining-room.

The rubbish was still in the fireplace, the chairs ranged along the wall. There were no dishes on the long table; but at the head of it two chairs; and at the foot, one; and in front of that, lying on the table, a folded bit of paper. Carmichael picked it up and opened it.

It was his prescription for the nitrite of amyl.

He hesitated a moment; then refolded the paper and put it in his vest-pocket.

Seated in his car, with his hand on the lever, he turned to Scudder, who was watching him with curious eyes.

"I'm very much obliged to you, Scudder, for taking me through the house. And I'll be more obliged to you if you'll just keep it to yourself—what I said to you about last night."

"Sure," said the old man, nodding gravely. "I like ye, doc', and that kinder talk might do ye harm here in Calvinton. We don't hold much to dreams and visions down this way. But, say, 'twas a mighty interestin' dream, wa'n't it? I guess Miss Jean hones for them white pillars, many a day—they sorter stand for old times. They draw ye, don't they?"

"Yes, my friend," said Carmichael as he moved the lever, "they speak of the past. There is a magic in those white pillars. They draw you."

THE EFFECTUAL FERVENT PRAYER

I

"O-o-o! Danny, oho-o-o! five o'clock!"

The clear young voice of Esther North floated across the snowy fields to the hill where the children of Glendour were coasting. Her brother Daniel, plodding up the trampled path beside the glairy track with half a dozen other boys, dragging the bob-sled on which his little sister Ruth was seated, heard the call with vague sentiments of dislike and rebellion. His twelve years rose up in arms against being ordered by a girl, even if she was sixteen and had begun to put up her hair and lengthen her skirts. She was a nice girl, to be sure—the prettiest in Glendour. But she might have had more sense than to call out that way before all the crowd. He had a good mind to pretend not to hear her.

But his comrades were not so minded. They had no idea of letting him evade the situation. They wanted him to stay, but he must do it like a man.

"Listen at your nurse already?" said one of the older lads mockingly; "she's a-callin' you. Run along home, boy!"

"Aw, no!" pleaded a youngster, not yet master of the art of irony. "Don't you mind her, Dan! The coast is just gettin' like glass, and you're the onliest one to steer the bob. You stay!"

"Please, Danny," said Ruth, keeping her seat as the sled stopped at the top of the hill, "only once more down! I ain't a bit tired."

"Dannee-ee-ee! O *Danny*!" came the sweet vibrant call again. "Five o'clock—come on—remember!"

Daniel remembered. The rules of the Rev. Nathaniel North's house were like the law of the Medes and Persians. Daniel had never met a Mede or a Persian, but in his mind he pictured them as persons with reddish-gray hair and beards and smooth-shaven upper lips, wearing white neckcloths and long black broadcloth coats, and requiring absolute punctuality at meal time, church time, school time, and family prayers. Esther's voice recalled him from the romance of the coasting-hill to the reality of life. He considered the consequences of being late for Saturday evening worship and made up his mind that they were too much for him.

"Come on, Ruthie," he cried, picking up the cord of her small sled, which she had forsaken for the greater glory and excitement of riding behind her brother on the bob. The child put her hand in his, and they ran together over the creaking snow to the place where their older sister was waiting, her slender figure in blue jacket and skirt outlined against the white field, and her golden hair shining like an aureole around her rosy face in the intense bloom of the winter sunset.

The three young Norths were the flower of Glendour: a Scotch village in western Pennsylvania, where the spirits of John Knox and Robert Burns lived face to face, separated by a great gulf. On one side of the street, near the river, was the tavern, where the lights burned late, and the music went to the tune of "Wandering Willie" and "John Barleycorn." On the other side of the street, toward the hills, was the Presbyterian church, where the sermons were an hour long, and the favourite lyric was

> *"A charge to keep I have."*

The Rev. Nathaniel North's "charge to keep" was the spiritual welfare of the elect, and especially of his own motherless children. To guide them in the narrow way, unspotted from the world, to train them up in the faith once delivered to the saints and in the customs which that faith had developed among the Scotch Covenanters, was the great desire of his heart. For that desire he would gladly have suffered martyrdom; and into the fulfilling of his task he threw a strenuous tenderness, a strong, unfaltering, sincere affection that bound his children to him by a love which lay far deeper than all their outward symptoms of restiveness under his strict rule.

This is a thing that seldom gets into stories. People of the world do not understand it. They are strangers to the intensity of religious passion, and to the swift instinct by which the heart of a child surrenders to absolute sincerity. This was what the North children felt in their father—a devotion that was grave, stern, almost fierce in its single-hearted attachment to them. He was theirs altogether. He would not let them dance or play cards. The theatre and even the circus were tabooed to them. Novel-reading was discouraged and no books were admitted to the house which had not passed under his censorship. All this seemed strange to them; they could not comprehend it; at times they talked together about the hardship of it—the two older ones—and made little plots to relax or circumvent the paternal rule. But in their hearts they accepted it, because they knew their father loved them better than any one else in the world, and they trusted him because they felt that he was a true man and a good man.

You see they were not "children in fiction"; they were real children—and beautiful, high-spirited children too. Esther was easily the "fairest of the village maids," and the head of her class in the high-school; Daniel, a leader in games among the boys of his age; even eight-year-old Ruth with her fly-away red hair and her wide brown eyes had her devoted admirers among the younger lads. It was evident to the Rev. Nathaniel North that his children were destined to have the perilous gift of popularity, and with all his natural pride in them he was tormented with anxiety on their account. How to protect them from temptation, how to shield them from the vain allurements of wealth and folly and fashion, how to surround them with an atmosphere altogether serious and devout and pure, how to keep them out of reach of the evil that is in the world—that was the tremendous problem upon which his mind and his heart laboured day and night.

Of course he admitted, or rather he positively affirmed, according to orthodox doctrine, that there was Original Sin in them. Under every human exterior, however fair, he postulated a heart "deceitful above all things and desperately wicked." This he regarded as a well-known axiom of theology, but it had no bearing at all upon the fact of experience that none of his children had ever lied to him, and that he would have been amazed out of measure if one of them should ever do a mean or a cruel thing. Yet he believed, all the same, that the mass of depravity must be there, in the nature which they inherited through him from Adam, like a heap of tinder, waiting for the fire. It was his duty to keep the fire from touching them, to guard them from the flame, even the spark, of worldliness. He gave thanks for his poverty which was like a wall about them. He prayed every night that no descendant of his might ever be rich. He was grateful for the seclusion and plainness of the village of Glendour in which vice certainly did not glitter.

"Separate from the world," he said to himself often; "that is a great mercy. No doubt there is evil here, as everywhere; but it is not gilded, it is not attractive. For my children's sake I am glad to live in obscurity, to keep them separate from the world."

But they were not conscious of any oppressive sense of separation as they walked homeward, through the saffron after-glow deepening into crimson and violet. The world looked near to them, and very great and beautiful, tingling with life even through its winter dress. The keen air, the crisp snow beneath their feet, the quivering stars that seemed to hang among the branches of the leafless trees, all gave them joy. They were healthily tired and heartily hungry; a good supper was just ahead of them, and beyond that a long life full of wonderful possibilities; and they were very glad to be alive. The two older children walked side by side pulling the sled with Ruth, who was willing to confess that she was "just a little mite tired" now that the fun was over.

"Esther," said the boy, "what do you suppose makes father so quiet and solemn lately—more than usual? Has anything happened, or is it just thinking?"

"Well," said the girl, who had a touch of the gentle tease in her, "perhaps it is just the left-over sadness from finding out that you'd been smoking!"

"Huh," murmured Dan, "you drop that, Essie! That was two weeks ago—besides, he didn't find out; I told him; and I took my medicine, too—never flinched. That's all over. More likely he remembers the fuss you made about not being let to go with the Slocums to see the theatre in Pittsburgh. You cried, baby! I didn't."

The boy rubbed the back of his hand reminiscently against the leg of his trousers, and Esther was sorry she had reminded him of a painful subject.

"Anyway," she said, "you had the best of it. I'd rather have gone, and told him about it, and taken a whipping afterward."

"What stuff! You know dad wouldn't whip a girl—not to save her life. Besides, when a thing's done, and 'fessed, and paid for, it's all over with dad. He's perfectly fair, I must say that. He doesn't nag like girls do."

"Now *you* drop *that*, Danny, and I'll tell you what I think is the matter with father. But you must promise not to speak to him about it."

"All right, I promise. What is it?"

"I guess—now mind, you mustn't tell—but I'm almost sure it is something about our Uncle Abel. A letter came last month, postmarked Colorado; and last week there was another letter in the same handwriting from Harrisburg. Father has been reading them over and over, and looking sadder each time. I guess perhaps Uncle Abel is in trouble or else— "

"You mean father's rich brother that lives out West? Billy Slocum told me about him once—says he's a king-pin out there, owns a mine a mile deep and full of gold, keeps lots of fast horses, wins races all over the country. He must be great. You mean him? Why doesn't father ever speak of him?"

The girl nodded her head and lowered her voice, glancing back to see that Ruth was not listening.

"You see," she continued, "father and Uncle Abel had a break—not a quarrel, but a kind of a divide—when they were young men. Lucy Slocum heard all about it from her grandmother, and told me. They were in a college scrape together, and father took his punishment, and after that he was converted, and you know how good he is. But his brother got mad, and he ran away from college, out West, and I reckon he has been—well, pretty bad. They say he gambled and drank and did all sorts of things. He said the world owed him a fortune and a good time. Now he's got piles of money and a great big place he calls Due North, with herds of cattle and ponies and a house full of pictures and things. I guess he's quieted down some, but he isn't married, and they say he isn't at all religious. He's what they call a free-thinker, and he just travels around with his horses and spends money. I suppose that is why father does not speak of him. You know he thinks that's all wrong, very wicked, and he wants to keep us separate from it all."

The boy listened to this long, breathless confidence in silence, kicking the lumps of snow in the road as he trudged along.

"Well," he said, "it seems kind of awful to have two brothers divided like that, doesn't it, Essie? But I suppose father's right, he 'most always is. Only I wish they'd make it up, and Uncle Abel would come here with some of his horses, and perhaps I could go West with him some time to make a start in life."

"Yes," added the girl, "and wouldn't it be fine to hear him tell about his adventures. And then perhaps he'd take an interest in us, and make things easier for father, and if he liked my singing he might give the money to send me to the Conservatory of Music. That would be great!"

"Yes," piped up the voice of Ruth from the sled, "and I wish he'd take us all out to Due North with him to see the ponies and the big house. That would be just lovely!"

Esther looked at Dan and smiled. Then she turned around.

"You little pitcher," she laughed, "what do you have such long ears for? But you must keep your mouth shut, anyway. Remember, I don't want you to speak to father about Uncle Abel."

"I didn't promise," said Ruth, shaking her head, "and I want him to come—it'll be better'n Santa Claus."

By this time the children had arrived at the little red brick parsonage, with its white wooden porch, on the side street a few doors back of the church. They stamped the snow off their feet, put the sled under the porch, hung their coats and hats in the entry, and went into the parlour on the stroke of half past five.

Over the mantel hung an engraving of "The Death-Bed of John Knox," which they never looked at if they could help it; on the opposite wall a copy of Reynolds's "Infant Samuel," which they adored. The pendent lamp, with a view of Jerusalem on the shade and glass danglers around the edge, shed a strong light on the marble-topped centre-table and the red plush furniture and the pale green paper with gilt roses on it.

On Saturday evening family worship came before supper. The cook and the maid-of-all-work were in their places on the smallest chairs, beside the door. On the sofa, where the children always sat, their Bibles were laid out. The father was in the big arm-chair by the centre-table with the book on his knees, already open.

The passage chosen was the last chapter of the Epistle of James. The deep, even voice of Nathaniel North sounded through that terrible denunciation of unholy riches with a gravity of conviction far more impressive than the anger of the modern muck-raker. The hearts of the children, remembering their conversation, were disturbed and vaguely troubled. Then came the gentler words about patience and pity and truthfulness and the healing of the sick. At the end each member of the house-hold was to read a sentence in turn and try to explain its meaning in a few words. The portion that fell to little Ruth was this:

"The effectual fervent prayer of a righteous man availeth much."

She stumbled over the two longer words, but she gave her comment clearly enough in her childish voice.

"That means if we obey Him, God will do anything we ask, I suppose."

The father nodded. "Right, my child. If we keep the commandments our prayers are sure of an answer. But remember that the people in the first part of the chapter have no such promise."

There was an unusual fervour in the prayer which closed the worship that night. Nathaniel North seemed to be putting his arms around the family to shield them from some unseen danger. The children, whose thoughts had wandered a little, while he was remembering the Jews and the heathen and the missionaries, in the customary phrases, felt their hearts dimly moved when he asked that his house might be kept from the power of darkness and the ravening wolves of sin, kept in unbroken purity and peace, holy and undefiled. The potent sincerity of his love came upon them. They believed with his faith; they consented with his will.

At the supper-table there was pleasant talk about books and school work and games and the plan to make a skating-pond in one of the lower fields that could be flooded after the snow had fallen. Nathaniel North, with all his strictness, was very near to his children; he wished to increase and to share their rightful happiness; he wanted them to be separate from the world but not from him. It was when they were talking of the coming school exhibition that Ruth dropped her little surprise into the conversation.

"Father," she said, "will Uncle Abel be here then? Oh, I wish he would come. I want to see him ever so much!"

He looked at her with astonishment for a moment. Esther and Daniel exchanged glances of dismay. They did not know what was coming. A serious rebuke from their father was not an easy thing to face. But when he spoke there was no rebuke in his voice.

"Children," he said, "it is strange that one of you should speak to me of my brother Abel when I have never spoken of him to you. But it is only natural, after all, and I should have foreseen it and been more frank with you. Have other people told you of him?"

"Oh, yes," they cried, with sparkling looks, but the father's face grew darker as he noticed their eagerness.

"Let me explain to you about him," he continued gravely. "He was my older brother—a year older—and as boys we were very fond of each other. But one day we had to part because our paths went in opposite directions. He chose the broad and easy way, and I was led into the straight and narrow path. How can two walk together except they be agreed? For ten years I tried to win him back, but without success. At last he told me that he wished me never to address him on the subject of religion again, for he would rather lose both his hands and his feet than believe as I did. He went on with his reckless life, prospering in this world, as I hear, but I have never seen him since that time."

"But wouldn't you like to see him?" said Esther, dropping her eyes. "He must be quite a wonderful man. Doesn't he write to you?"

Her father's lip twitched, but he still spoke sadly and gravely.

"I see you have guessed the answer already. Yes, a letter came from him some time ago, proposing a visit, which I discouraged. Another came this week, saying that he was on his way, driving his own horses across the country, and though he had received no reply from me, he hoped to get here late Saturday—that is, to-night—or Sunday morning. Of course we must welcome my own brother—if he comes."

"Why, he may get here any minute," cried Daniel eagerly; "he's sure to change his wagon for a sleigh in Pittsburgh, and he won't have to drive 'way round by the long bridge, he can cross the river on the ice. I wonder if he's driving that famous long-distance team that Slocum told me about. Oh, that'll be simply great."

"I must go upstairs right away," exclaimed Esther, with brightening face, "to see that the guest room is ready for him when he comes."

"I'll go to help" cried Ruth, clapping her hands. "What fun to have a real uncle here. I guess he'll bring a present for each of us."

"Wait, my children," said the father, lifting his hand, "before you go I have something more to say to you. Your uncle is a man of the world, and you know the world is evil; we have been called to come out of it. He does not think as we do, nor believe as we do, nor live as we do, according to the Word. For one thing, he cares nothing for the sanctity of the Sabbath. Unless he has changed very much, he is not temperate nor reverent. I fear the effect of his example in Glendour. I fear his influence upon you, my children. It is my duty to warn you, to put you on your guard. It will be a hard trial. But we must receive him—if he comes."

"If he comes?" cried Esther, evidently alarmed; "there's no doubt of that, is there, since he has written?"

"My dear, when you know your uncle you will understand that there is always a doubt. He is very irregular and uncertain in all his ways. He may change his mind or be turned aside. No one can tell. But go to your tasks now, my children, and to bed early. I have some work to do in my study."

Each of them kissed him good-night, and he watched them out of the room with a look of tender sternness in his lined and rugged face, anxious, troubled, and ready to give his life to safeguard them from the invisible arrows of sin. Then he went into his long, narrow book-room, but not to work.

Up and down the worn and dingy carpet, between the walls lined with dull grey and brown and black books, he paced with heavy feet. The weight of a dreadful responsibility pressed upon him, the anguish of a spiritual conflict tore his heart. His old affection for his brother seemed to revive and leap up within him, like a flame from smothered embers when the logs are broken open. The memory of their young comradeship and joys together grew bright and warm. He longed to see Abel's face once more.

Then came other memories, dark and cold, crowding in upon him with evil faces to chill and choke his love. The storm of rebellion that led to the parting, the wild and reckless life in the far country, the gambling, the drinking, the fighting, the things that he knew and the things that he guessed—and then, the ways of Abel when he returned, at times, in the earlier years, with his pockets full of money to spend it in the worst company and with a high-handed indifference to all restraint, yet always with a personal charm of generosity and good-will that drew people to him and gave him a strange power over them—and then, Abel's final refusal to listen any more to the pleadings of the true faith, his good-humoured obstinacy in unbelief, his definite choice of the world as his portion, and after that the long silence and the growing rumours of his wealth, his extravagance, his devotion, if not to the lust of the flesh, at least to the lust of the eyes and the pride of life—all these thoughts and pictures rushed upon Nathaniel North and overwhelmed him with painful terror and foreboding. They seemed to loom above him and his children like black clouds charged with hidden disaster. They shook his sick heart with an agony of trembling hatred.

He did not hate his brother—no, never that—and there was the poignant pain of it. The bond of affection rooted in his very flesh, held firm and taut, stretched to the point of anguish, and vibrating in shrill notes of sorrow as the hammer of conviction struck it. He could not cast his brother out of his inmost heart, blot his name from the book of remembrance, cease to hope that the infinite mercy might some day lay hold upon him before it was too late.

But the things for which that brother stood in the world—the ungodliness, the vainglory, the material glitter and the spiritual darkness—these things the minister was bound to hate; and the more he hated the more he feared and trembled. The intensity of this fear seemed for the time to blot out all other feelings. The coming of such a man, with all his attractions, with the glamour of his success, with the odours and enchantments of the world about him, was an incalculable peril. The pastor agonised for his flock, the father for his little ones. It seemed as if he saw a tiger with glittering eyes creeping near and crouching for a spring. It seemed as if a serpent, with bright colours coiled and fatal head poised, were waiting in the midst of the children for one of them to put out a hand to touch it. Which would it be? Perhaps all of them would be fascinated. They were so eager, so innocent, so full of life. How could he guard them in a peril so subtle and so terrible?

He had done all that he could for them, but perhaps it was not enough. He felt his weakness, his helpless impotence. They would slip away from him and be lost—perhaps forever. Already his sick heart saw them charmed, bewildered, poisoned, perishing in ways where his imagination shuddered to follow them.

The torture of his love and terror crushed him. He sank to his knees beside the ink-stained wooden table on the threadbare carpet and buried his face in his arms. All of his soul was compressed into a single agony of prayer.

He prayed that this bitter trial might not come upon him, that this great peril might not approach his children. He prayed that the visitation which he dreaded might be averted by almighty power. He prayed that God would prevent his brother from coming, and keep the home in unbroken purity and peace, holy and undefiled.

From this strange wrestling in spirit he rose benumbed, yet calmed, as one who feels that he has made his last effort and can do no more. He opened the door of his study and listened. There was no sound. The children had all gone to bed. He turned back to the old table to work until midnight on his sermon for the morrow. The text was: "*As for me and my house, we will serve the Lord.*"

II

But that sermon was not to be delivered. Mr. North woke very early, before it was light, and could not find sleep again. In the gray of the morning, when the little day was creeping among the houses of Glendour, he heard steps in the street and then a whisper of voices at his gate. He threw his wrapper around him and went down quietly to open the door.

A group of men were there, with trouble in their faces. They told him of an accident on the river. A sleigh crossing the ice during the night had lost the track. The horses had broken into an air-hole and dragged the sleigh with them. The man went under the ice with the current, and came out a little while ago in the big spring-hole by the point. They had pulled the body ashore. They did not know for sure who it was—a stranger—but they thought—perhaps——

The minister listened silently, shivering once or twice, and passing his hand over his brow as if to brush away something. When their voices paused and ceased, he said slowly, "Thank you for coming to me. I must go with you, and then I can tell." As he went upstairs softly and put on his clothes, he repeated these words to himself two or three times mechanically—"yes, then I can tell." But as he went with the men he said nothing, walking like one in a dream.

On the bank of the river, amid the broken ice and trampled yellow snow, the men had put a couple of planks together and laid the body of the stranger upon them turning up the broad collar of his fur coat to hide his face. One of the men now turned the collar down, and Nathaniel North looked into the wide-open eyes of the dead.

A horrible tremor shook him from head to foot. He lifted his hands, as if he must cry aloud in anguish. Then suddenly his face and figure seemed to congeal and stiffen with some awful inward coldness—the frost of the last circle of the Inferno—it spread upon him till he stood like a soul imprisoned in ice.

"Yes," he said, "this is my brother Abel. Will you carry him to my house? We must bury him."

During the confusion and distress of the following days that frozen rigidity never broke nor melted. Mr. North gave no directions for the funeral, took no part in it, but stood beside the grave in dreadful immobility. He did not mourn. He did not lament. He listened to his friends' consolation as if it were spoken in an unknown tongue. Nothing helped him, nothing hurt, because nothing touched him. He did no work, opened no book, spoke no word if he could avoid it. He moved about his house like a stranger, a captive, shrinking from his children so that they grew afraid to come close to him. They were bewildered and harrowed with pity. They did not know what to do. It seemed as if it were their father and not their uncle who had died.

Every attempt to penetrate the ice of his anguish failed. He gave no sign of why or how he suffered. Most of the time he spent alone in his book-room, sitting with his hands in his lap, staring at the unspeakable thought that paralysed him, the thought that was entangled with the very roots of his creed and that glared at him with monstrous and malignant face above the very altar of his religion—the thought of his last prayer—the effectual prayer, the fervent prayer, the damnable prayer that branded his soul with the mark of Cain, his brother's murderer.

The physician grew alarmed. He feared the minister would lose his reason in a helpless melancholia. The children were heart-broken. All their efforts to comfort and distract their father fell down hopeless from the mask of ice, behind which they saw him like a spirit in prison. Daniel and Ruth were ready to give up in despair. But Esther still clung to the hope that she could do something to rescue him.

One night, when the others had gone to bed, she crept down to the sombre study. Her father did not turn his head as she entered. She crossed the room and knelt down by the ink-stained table, laying her hands on his knee. He put them gently away and motioned her to rise.

"Do not do that," he said in a dull voice.

She stood before him, wringing her hands, the tears streaming down her face, but her voice was sweet and steady.

"Father," she said, "you must tell me what it is that is killing you. Don't you know it is killing us too? Is it right for you to do that? I know it is something more than uncle's death that hurts you. It is sad to lose a brother, but there is something deeper in your heart. Tell me what it is. I have the right to know. I ask you for mother's sake."

He lifted his head and looked at her. His eyelids quivered. His secret dragged downward in his breast like an iron hand clutching his throat-strings. His voice was stifled. But no matter what it cost him, to her, the first child of his love, his darling, he must speak at last.

"You have the right to know, Esther," he said, with a painful effort. "I will tell you what is in my soul. I killed my brother Abel. The night of his death, I knelt at that table and prayed that he might be prevented from coming to this house. My only thought, my only wish was that he must be kept away. That was all I asked for. God killed him because I asked it. His blood is on my soul."

He leaned back in his chair exhausted, and shut his eyes.

The girl stood dazed for a moment, struck dumb by the grotesque horror of what she had heard. Then the light of Heaven-sent faith flashed through her and the courage of human love warmed her. She sprang to her father, sobbing, almost laughing in the joy of triumph. She flung herself across his knees and put her arms around him.

"Father, did you teach us that God is our Father, our real Father?"

The man did not answer, but the girl went bravely on:

"Father, if I asked you to kill Ruth, would you do it?"

The man stirred a little, but he did not open his eyes nor answer, and the girl went bravely on:

"Father, is it fair to God to believe that He would do something that you would be ashamed of? Isn't He better than you are?"

The man opened his eyes. The light of his old faith kindled in them. He answered firmly:

"He is infinite, absolute, and unchangeable. His Word is sure. We dare not question Him. There is the promise—the effectual fervent prayer of a righteous man availeth much."

The girl did not look up. She clung to him more closely and buried her face on his breast.

"Yes, father dear, but if what you asked in your prayer was wrong, were you a righteous man? Could your prayer have any power?"

It was her last stroke—she trembled as she made it. There was a dead silence in the room. She heard the slow clock ticking on the mantel, the wind whistling in the chimney. Then her father's breast was shaken, his head fell upon her shoulder, his tears rained upon her neck.

"Thank God," he cried, "I was a sinner—it was not a prayer—God be merciful to me a sinner!"

THE RETURN OF THE CHARM

I

"Nor I," cried John Harcourt, pulling up in the moon-silvered mist and clapping his hand to his pocket, "not a groat! Stay, here is a crooked sixpence of King James that none but a fool would take. The merry robbers left me that for luck."

Dick Barton growled as he turned in his saddle. "We must ride on, then, till we find a cousin to loan us a few pounds. Sir Empty-purse fares ill at an inn."

"By my sore seat," laughed Harcourt, "we'll ride no farther to-night. Here we 'light, at the sign of the Magpie in the Moon. The rogues of Farborough Cross have trimmed us well; the honest folk of Market Farborough shall feed us better!"

"For a crooked sixpence!" grumbled Barton. "Will you beg our entertainment like a pair of landlopers, or will you take it by force like our late friends on the road?"

"Neither," said Harcourt, "but in the fashion that befits gentlemen—with a bold face, a gay tongue, and a fine coat well carried. Remember, Dick, look up, and no snivelling! Tell your ill-fortune and you bid for more. 'Tis Monsieur Debonair that owns the tavern."

Their lusty shouts brought the hostler on the trot to take their steaming horses, and the landlord stood in the open door, his broad face a welcome to such handsome guests. They entered as if the place belonged to them, and called for the best it contained as if it were just good enough. The whole house was awake and astir with their coming. The smiling maids ran to and fro; the rustics in the long room stared and admired: the table was spread with a fair cloth and loaded with a smoking supper; and afterward there were pots of ale for all the company, and a song with a chorus. The landlord, with his thumbs in the arm-holes of his waistcoat, patted himself to see his business go so merrily. But the landlady came to the door, now and then, and looked in with anxious eyes.

"Mark the mistress," whispered Barton; "she has her suspicions."

"Her troubles," answered Harcourt, "and that I relish not. I will have all happy around me, else my spirit sinks and the game is lost. I'll talk with her."

He beckoned her to his side with a courteous gesture.

"A famous supper, Mistress," said he, "but your face is too downcast for the maker of such a masterpiece. What is it that ails you?"

"It is my child," she answered; "kind sir, my little Faith is ill of fever, and the physician has been called away. He has left her a draught, but she grows worse, and the fever holds her from sleep. It may be that you know something of the healing art."

"As much as any man," said Harcourt, confidently. "You see in me, despite my youth, a practitioner of the oldest school in the world, a disciple of Galen's grandfather. Let me go with you to look at the child."

The little girl lay in a close room. Her curls were tangled on the pillow and her thin, brown arms tossed on the hot counterpane. By her side was a glass of some dark medicine, and her black eyes held more of rebellion than of fever as she gazed at the stranger.

He leaned over her with a smile, smoothing her wrists lightly, with slow, downward touches, and whispering in her ear. The sound of the singing below came through the door ajar, and the child listened to her visitor as if he were telling her a wonderful tale.

"Open the window," he said, after a while, to the mother, pulling the sheet softly over the child's shoulders, "the air to-night is full of silver threads which draw away the fever."

Then he threw the black draught out of the window. And the child, watching him, laughed a little.

"It is the wrong medicine," said he. "Bring me paper and pen."

He wrote by the light of the flickering candle, hiding the words with his other hand: *Fortune favour Faith.*

Then he slipped the crooked sixpence into the paper, folded it carefully, tucking the ends one into the other, and marked it with a cross.

"Hold it tight," he said to the child, closing the fingers of her right hand upon the little packet. "It will let you into the Garden of Good Dreams. And now your carriage is ready, and now your horses are trotting, gently, gently, quickly, softly along the white moon-road to the Land of Nod. Will you go—are you going—are you gone?"

Her eyelids drooped and fell, and she turned on her right side with a sigh, thrusting her brown fist under the pillow. Harcourt drew the mother to the door.

"Hush," he whispered; "leave the window wide. Your Faith holds an ancient potent charm, thousands of years old, better than all medicines. Do not speak of it to any one. If you open it, you will lose it. Let her sleep with it so, and bring it me on the morrow."

In the morning, when the landlord had served breakfast with his own hands, Harcourt called boldly for the bill; and Barton stared at him, but the landlord was confused.

"My wife," he stammered—"you must excuse her, gentlemen, nothing will do but she must speak with you herself about the reckoning. I'll go call her."

She came with a wonder of gladness in her face, and the little girl clinging to a fold of her mother's dress by the left hand and pressing the other brown fist close to her neck.

"You see," said the mother. "She is well! Run, Faith, and kiss the gentleman's hand. Oh, sir, there can be no talk of payment between us—we are deep in your debt; but if my child might keep this ancient potent charm?"

The question hung in her voice. Harcourt delayed a moment, as if in doubt, before he answered, smiling:

"I am loath to part from it," he said at last, "but since she has proved it, let her keep it and believe in it for good—never for evil. Come, little Faith, kiss me good-bye—no, not on the hand!"

When they were alone together, Barton turned upon his companion with reproachful looks.

"What is this charm?" he asked.

"A secret," answered the other curtly.

"I like it not," said Barton, shaking his head; "you go too far, Jack. You put a deception on these simple folk."

"Who knows?" laughed Harcourt. "At least I have done them no harm. We leave them happy and ride on. How far to your nearest cousin?"

II

"The next case is a strange one," said Sir Richard Barton, Justice of the Peace, sitting on the bench by his friend, the famous Judge who was holding court for Market Farborough.

"How is it strange?" asked the Judge, whose face showed ruddy and strong beneath his white wig.

"It is an accusation of witchcraft," answered Sir Richard, "and that is a serious thing in these days. Yet it seems the woman has a good heart and harms nobody."

"Beneficent witchcraft!" said the Judge—"that is a rarity indeed. What do you make of it?"

"I am against all superstition," said Sir Richard solemnly; "it brings disorder. For religion we have the clergy, and for justice the lawyers, and for health the doctors. All outside of that partakes of license and unreason."

"Yet outside of that," mused the Judge, "there are things that neither clergy nor lawyers nor doctors can explain. Tell me, what do people think concerning this witch?"

"The strict and godly folk," answered Sir Richard, "reckon her a scandal to the town and an enemy of religion. They are of opinion that she should be put away, whether by hanging or drowning, or by shutting her in a madhouse. But many poor people have an affection for her, because she has helped them."

"And you?" asked the Judge.

Sir Richard looked at him keenly. "I can better tell," said he, "when you have seen her yourself and heard her story."

"That is plainly my duty," said the Judge. "Clerk, call the next case."

As the clerk read the name of the accused and the charge against her, the eyes of the Judge were fixed curiously upon the prisoner at the bar, as if he sought for something forgotten.

Tall and dark, with sunburned face and fearless eyes, she stood quietly while her way of life was told; her dwelling, since the death of her parents, in a cottage on the heath beyond the town; her comings and goings among the neighbours; her wonderful cures of sick animals and strange diseases, but especially of little children. There were some who testified that she was wilful and malicious; yet it appeared they could only allege she had withheld her cure, saying that it was beyond her power. The doctor was bitter against her, as an unlawful person; and the parson condemned her, though she came often to church; "for," said he, "the Scripture commands us, 'Thou shalt not suffer a witch to live.'"

The face of the Judge was troubled. "Tell me," he said, leaning forward and speaking gravely, "are you a witch?"

"Not for evil, my Lord," answered the woman simply, "but I have a healing gift."

"How do you work your cures?" he asked. "What do you to the children?"

"I open the windows of the room where they lie," she answered.

The face of the Judge relaxed, and his eyes twinkled kindly. "And then?" said he.

"I throw the black draught out of the window and tell the children a tale of the Garden of Good Dreams."

"Is that all?" said the Judge, shading his face with his hand.

"No, my Lord," replied the woman. "When the children are near to sleep, I put my charm in their hands."

"Whence had you this charm?" he said. "And what is it?"

"I pray your Lordship," cried the woman, "ask me not, for I can never tell."

"Let me see it," said the Judge, with a smile.

So the woman, trembling and reluctant, drew a dark-red ribbon from her breast, and at the end of it a packet of fine linen bound closely with white silk. She laid it before the Judge. He broke the silken thread and unrolled the linen, fold after fold, until he came to a yellow piece of paper with writing on it, and in the paper a crooked sixpence of King James.

The coin and the scrap of paper lay in his hand as he looked up and met the shrewd questioning eyes of Sir Richard.

"Yes," answered the Baron Harcourt in a low voice, "you have seen the coin before, and now you may read what is written on the paper."

"Now I know," said Sir Richard, shaking his head, "what charm you gave to the woman and her child forty years ago. Was I not right? It was a deception."

"Who knows?" said the Baron Harcourt cheerfully. "It has not failed to-day. Fortune has favoured Faith."

He turned to the clerk. "Make record that this case is dismissed for want of evidence against the accused. The woman has done no harm. The court is adjourned."

"And my charm," said the woman eagerly—"oh, my Lord, you will give me back my charm?"

"That I must keep for you," he said with kindness, as to a child. "But you may still open the windows, and throw out the black draught, and tell the children of the Garden of Good Dreams. Trust me, that will work wonders."

HALF-TOLD TALES: BEGGARS UNDER THE BUSH

As I came round the bush I was aware of four beggars in the shade of it, counting their spoils.

They sat at their ease, with food and a flagon of wine before them and silver cups, for all the world like gentlefolk on a picnic, only happier. But I knew them for beggars by the boldness of their asking eyes and the crook in their fingers.

They looked at me curiously, as if to say, “What do you bring us?”

“Nothing, gentlemen,” I answered, “I am only seeking information.”

At this they moved uneasily and glanced at one another with a crafty look of alarm. Their crooked fingers closed around the cups.

“Are you a collector of taxes?” cried the first beggar.

“Certainly not,” I replied with heat, “but a payer of them!”

“Come, come,” said the beggar, with a wink at his comrades, “no insult intended! Only a prudent habit of ours in these days of mixed society. But you are evidently poor and honest. Take a chair on the grass. Honesty we love, and to poverty we have no objection—in fact, we admire it—in others.”

So I sat down beside them in the shade of the bush and lit my pipe to listen.

In the hot field below, a man was ploughing amid the glare of the sun. The reins hung about his neck like a halter, and he clung to the jerking handles of the plough while the furrows of red earth turned and fell behind him like welts on the flank of the hill.

“A hard life,” said the second beggar, draining his cup, “but healthy! And very useful! The world must have bread.”

“Plenty of it,” said the third beggar, “else what would become of that?”

He nodded down the valley, where tall spires pointed toward the blue and taller chimneys veiled it with black. The huddled city seemed to move and strain and quiver under the dusky curtain, and the fumes of its toil hung over it like steam from a sweating horse.

“It is a sad sight,” said the fourth beggar, waving his hand with the gesture of an orator. “Shakespeare was right when he said, ‘God made the country and man made the town.’ Admit for the present that cities are necessary evils. The time is coming when every man must have his country-place. Meanwhile let us cultivate the rural virtues.”

He smacked his lips and lifted the flagon.

“Right,” said the first beggar, “a toast! To the simple life!”

So the four quaffed a cupful of wine—and I a puff of smoke—to the simple life.

In the bush was a bird, very busy catching flies. He perched on a branch, darted into the air, caught his fly, and fluttered to another branch. Between flies he chirped and twittered cheerfully.

"Beautiful bird," said the first beggar, leaning back, "a model of cheerful industry! What do they call him?"

"A warbler," said I, "because he has so little voice."

"He might sing better," observed the second beggar, "if he did not work so hard catching flies."

But the fourth beggar sighed and wiped the corner of his left eye, for he was a tender-hearted man on one side.

"I am thinking," said he, "of the poor flies!"

"Bet you a hundred to ten he doesn't catch the next one," said the third beggar.

"Done," cried the others, but before the stakes were counted out, the bird had flown.

"Tell me, sirs," I began, when they had stripped the gilded bands from their cigars and lighted them, "what it is that makes you all so innocently merry and contented in this troublous world?"

"It is a professional secret," said the first beggar. "If we tell it, you will give it away."

"Never," I answered. "I only want to put it into a poem."

The beggars looked at one another and laughed heartily. "That will do no harm," said they, "our secret will be safe there."

"Well, then," said the first beggar gravely, "it is religion. We approve the conduct of Providence. It must be all right. The Lord is on our side. It would be wicked to ask why. We practise the grace of resignation, and find peace."

"No," said the second beggar smiling, "religion is an old wives' tale. It is philosophy that makes us contented. Nothing could be unless it was, and nothing is different from what it has to be. Evolution goes on evolving all the time. So here we are, you see, in the best world possible at the present moment. Why not make the most of it? Pass me the flagon."

"Not at all," interrupted the fourth beggar loudly, "I will have none of your selfish religion or your immoral philosophy. I am a Reformer. This is the worst world possible, and that is why I enjoy it. It gives me my chance to make orations about reform. Philanthropy is the secret of happiness."

"Piffle!" said the third beggar, tossing a gold coin in the air. "You talk as if people heard you. The secret of happiness—religion, philosophy, philanthropy?—poppycock! It is luck, sheer luck. Life is a game of chance. Heads I win, tails you lose. Will you match me, Master Poet?"

"You will have to excuse me," I said. "I have only a penny in my pocket. But I am still puzzled by your answers. You seem of many minds, but of one spirit. You are all equally contented. How is this?"

The eyes of the beggars turned to the piles of booty in front of them, and they all nodded their heads wisely as if to say, "you can see."

A packet of papers lay before the first beggar and his look lingered on them with love.

"How came you by these?" I asked.

"An old gentleman gave them to me," he answered. "He said he was my grandfather. He was an unpleasant old fellow, but God rest his soul! These are all gilt-edged."

The second beggar was playing with a heap of jewels. He was a handsome fellow with fine hands.

"How did you get these pretty things?" said I.

"By consenting to be married," he replied. "It was easy enough. She squints, and her grammar is defective, but she is a good little thing."

The third beggar ran his fingers through the pile of gold before him, and took up a coin, now and then, to flip it in the air.

"How did you earn this?" I asked.

"Earn it!" said he scornfully, "do you take me for a labouring man? These fellows here lent me something, and I bet on how much corn that fellow down there with the plough would raise—and the rest—why, the rest was luck, sheer luck!"

"And you?" I turned to the fourth beggar who had a huge bag beside him, so full of silver that the dimes and quarters ran from the mouth of it.

"I," said he loftily, "am a Reformer. The people love me and give me whatever I want, because I tell them that these other beggars have no right to their money. I am going to be President."

At this they all burst into shouts of laughter and rolled on the grass. Even the Reformer chuckled a little.

While they were laughing, the ploughman came up with an axe and began to chop at the bush.

"What are you doing to our bush?" cried the beggars.

"Chopping it down," said the ploughman.

"But why?" cried they.

"I must plough this field," said he.

So the beggars grabbed their spoils and scuttled away to other countries, and I went on over the hill.

HALF-TOLD TALES: STRONGHOLD

It rose upon the rock like a growth of nature; secure, commanding, imperturbable; mantled with ivy and crowned with towers; a castle of the olden time, called Stronghold.

Below it, the houses of the town clung to the hillside, creeping up close to the castle wall and clustering in its shadow as if to claim protection. In truth, for many a day it had been their warden against freebooter and foreign foe, gathering the habitations of the humble as a hen gathers her chickens beneath her wings to defend them from the wandering hawk.

But those times of disorder and danger were long past. The roaming tribes had settled down in their conquered regions. The children of the desert had learned to irrigate their dusty fields. The robber chiefs had sobered into merchants and money-lenders. The old town by the river had a season of peace, labouring and making merry and sleeping and bringing forth children and burying its dead in tranquillity, protected by forts far away and guarded by ships on distant waters.

Yet Stronghold still throned upon the rock, proudly dominant; and the houses full of manifold life were huddled at its foot; and the voices of men and women and little children, talking or laughing or singing or sobbing or cursing or praying, went up around it like smoke.

Now the late lord of the castle, in the last age of romance, had carried off a beautiful peasant girl with dove's eyes, whom he married on her death-bed where she gave birth to their son. The blood of his father and of his mother met in the boy's body, and in his soul their spirits were mingled, so that he was by times haughty and gentle, and by turns fierce and tender, and he grew up a dreamer with sudden impulses to strong action. To him, at his father's death, fell the lordship of the castle; and he was both proud and thoughtful; and he considered the splendour of his ancient dwelling and the duties of his high station.

The doors of Stronghold, at this time, were always open, not only for the going out of the many retainers and servants on their errands of business and mercy and pleasure in the town, but also for the citizens and the poor folk who came seeking employment, or demanding justice, or asking relief for their necessities. The lord of the castle had ordered that none should be denied, and that a special welcome should be given to those who came with words of enlightenment and counsel, to interpret the splendour of Stronghold and help its master to learn the duties of his high station.

So there came many men with various words. Some told him of the days when Stronghold was the defence of the land and the foreign foe was broken against it. Some walked with him in the long hall of portraits and narrated the brave deeds of his ancestors. Some explained to him the history of the heirlooms, and showed him how each vessel of silver and great carved chair and richly faded tapestry had a meaning which made it precious.

Other men talked to him of the future and of the things that he ought to do. They set forth new schemes of industry by which the castle should be changed into a central power-house or a silk-mill. They unfolded new plans of bounty by which the hungry should be clad, and the naked fed, and the sick given an education. They told him that if he would do these things, in the course of a hundred years or so all would be well.

But the trouble was that their counsels were contradictory, and their promises were distant, and the lord of the castle was impatient and bewildered in mind. For meantime the manifold voices of the town went up around him like smoke, and he knew that underneath it some fires of trouble and sorrow must be burning.

Then came two barefaced and masterful men who told him bluntly that the first duty of his high station was to abandon it.

"What shall I do then?" he asked.

"Work for your living," they shouted.

"What do you do for your living?" he inquired.

"We tell other men what to do," replied they.

"And do you think," said he, "that your job is any harder than mine, or that you work more than I do?" So he gave order that they should have a good supper and be escorted from the castle, for he had no time to waste upon mummers.

But the confusion in his mind continued, because the spirits of his father and his mother were working within him, and the impulse to sudden action gathered force beneath his dreams. So he was glad when the next visitor came bearing the marks of evident sincerity and a great purpose.

His beard was untrimmed, his garb was rude, his feet were bare, like an ancient prophet. His voice was fiercely quiet, and his eyes burned while he talked, as if he saw to the root of all things. He called himself John the Nothingarian.

The lord of the castle related some of the plans which his counsellors had made for his greater usefulness.

"They are puerile," said the Nothingarian, "futile, because they do not go to the root."

Then the young lord spoke of the legends of his forefathers and the history of Stronghold.

"They are dusty tales," said the Nothingarian, "false, because they do not go to the root."

"How shall we get to the root?" asked the young lord, trembling with a new eagerness.

"There is only one way," answered the prophet. "Come with me."

As they went through the outer passageway the old man pressed hard with his hands against one of the stones in the wall, and a little door slid open.

"The secret stair," said he, "by which your fathers brought in their stolen women. Your Stronghold is honeycombed with lies."

The young lord's face was red as fire. "I never knew of it," he murmured.

In the vaulted crypt beneath the castle the old man found a lantern and a pickaxe. He went to an alcove walled with plaster and picked at it with the axe. The plaster fell away. On the floor of the alcove lay two crumpled bodies of men long dead; the clothes were rotting upon the bones and a dagger stuck fast in each back.

"They were stabbed as they sat at meat," said the old man, "for the gain of their gold. Your Stronghold is cemented with blood."

The young lord's face grew dark as night. "I never knew of it," he muttered.

"Come," said the other, "I see we must go a little deeper before you know where you stand."

So he led the way through the long vaults, where the cobwebs trailed like rags and the dripping pendules of lime hung from the arches like dirty icicles, until he came to the foundation of the great tower. There he set down the lantern and began to dig, fiercely and silently, close to the corner-stone, throwing out the rubble with his bare hands. At last the pick broke through into a hollow niche. At the bottom of it was the skeleton of a child about five years old, and the cords that bound her little hands and feet lay in white dust upon the sunken bones.

"You see!" said the old man, wiping his torn hands on his robe. "The corner-stones were laid for safety on the body of a murdered innocent. Your Stronghold is founded on cruelty. This is the root."

The young lord's face went white as death. "Horrible!" he cried. "But what to do?"

"Do away with it!" said the Nothingarian. "That is the only thing. Come!"

He went out into the night and the young lord followed him, the sudden impulse to strong action leaping in his heart and pounding in his temples and ringing in his ears, like a madness.

They passed around behind the great tower, where it stood close to the last pinnacle of the rock and rose above it, bolted to the high crest of stone by an iron bar.

"Here is the clutch of your Stronghold," said the old man urgently. "Break that and all goes down. Dare you strike to the root?"

"I dare," he cried, "for I must. A thing built on cruelty, cemented with blood, and worm-eaten with lies is hateful to me as to God."

He lifted the pick and struck. Once! and the castle trembled to its base and the servants ran out at the doors. Twice! and the tower swayed and a cry of fear arose. Thrice! and the huge walls of Stronghold rocked and crashed and thundered down upon the sleeping town, burying it in wild ruin!

Dead silence for an instant—and then, through the cloud of dust that hung above the flattened houses, came a lamentable tumult. Voices of men and women and little children, shrieking in fear, groaning with pain, whimpering for pity, moaning in mortal anguish, rose like smoke from the pit beneath the wreck of Stronghold.

The young lord listened, dizzy and sick with horror. Then he looked at the Nothingarian whose eyes glittered wildly. He swung up the pickaxe again.

"Curse you," he cried, "why didn't you tell me of this?" And he split his head down to the beard.

HALF-TOLD TALES: IN THE ODOUR OF SANCTITY

Mortem suscepit cantando[1]

Last of all, the crouching plague leaped upon the Count Angelo (whose women and boon companions already lay dead around him in his castle of Montefeltro), and dragged him from the banquet-hall of many delights into the dim alley of the grave. There he looked, as it were through a door half open, into the shapeless horror of the face of Death, which turns all desires into stone. But even while he looked, the teeth of the black beast that gripped him were loosened, and he crept back into life as one returning from a far country.

His castle was empty save for the few terror-stricken servants who lingered because they knew not whither to flee. In the garden withered the rose and the lily, untended and unplucked. The chairs and couches where he had seen the faces of his friends were vacant. On the pillows of his great bed there were no curls of tangled gold, nor plaited tresses of long black spread out beside him in the morning light.

The world in which he had revelled away his youth was void; and in the unknown world, from whose threshold he had painfully escaped, but whither he knew he must one day return, there dwelt only a horrible fear and a certain looking for of judgment.

So Count Angelo came to life again. But all desires and passions which had hitherto warmed or burned him were like dead embers. For the flame of them all had gone into one desire—the resolve to die in the odour of sanctity, and so to pass into Paradise safely and unafraid.

Therefore he put aside the fine garments which his trembling servants brought, and clad himself in sackcloth with a girdle of rope about his loins. Thus apparelled he climbed on foot to the holy mountain of La Verna, above the Val d'Arno, which mountain the Count Rolando of Montefeltro had given, many years before, to St. Francis the minstrel of God and his poor little disciples of the cross, for a refuge and a sanctuary near the sky. At the door of the Friary built upon the land of his forefathers the Count Angelo knocked humbly as a beggar.

"Who is there?" said the door-keeper from his loophole.

"A poor sinner," answered Angelo, "who has no wish left in life but to die in the odour of sanctity."

---

1 Death with singing.

At this the door-keeper opened grudgingly, supposing he had to do with some outcast seeking the house of religion as a last resort. But when he saw the stranger he knew that it was the rich and generous Count of Montefeltro.

"May it please your lordship to enter," he cried; "the guest-chamber awaits you, and the friars minor of St. Francis will rejoice in the presence of their patron."

"Not so," replied Angelo; "but in the meanest of your cells will I lodge. For I am come not to bestow, but to beg, and my request is the lowest place among the little servants of poverty."

Whereupon the door-keeper was greatly astonished, and led Angelo to the Warden, to whom he unfolded his purpose to strip himself of all worldly gear and possessions and give his remnant of life solely to the preparation of a saintly death. This proposal the Warden and the other brethren duly considered, not without satisfaction, and Angelo was received as a penitent and a novice.

The first year of his probation he passed as a servant of the cattle and the beasts of burden, cleansing their stables and conversing only with them. "For," said he, "the ox and the ass knew their Lord in the manger, but I in my castle was deaf to his voice."

The second year of his probation he laboured in the kitchen, washing the dishes and preparing the food for the friars, but he himself ate sparingly and only of the crusts and crumbs which the others had despised. "For," said he, "I am less worthy than that lad who brought the few loaves and small fishes to feed the multitude, and for me it is enough to eat of the fragments that remain."

In all this he was so diligently humble and self-denying that in the third year he was admitted fully to the order and given the honourable office of sweeping and cleansing the sacred places.

In this duty Angelo showed an extraordinary devotion. Not content with this, he soon began to practise upon himself particular and extreme asperities and macerations. He slept only upon the ground and never beyond an hour at one space, rising four and twenty times a day to his prayers. He fasted thrice in the week from matins to matins, and observed the rule of silence every six days, speaking only on the seventh. He wore next to his naked skin a breastplate of iron, and a small leather band with sharp points about his loins, and rings of iron under his arms, whereby his flesh was wasted and frayed from his bones like a worn garment with holes in it, and he bled secretly. By reason of these things his face fell away into a dolorous sadness, and the fame of his afflictions spread through the Friary and to other houses where the little brothers of St. Francis were assembled.

But the inward gladness of Angelo did not increase in measure with his outward sadness and the renown of his piety. For the ray and the flame of divine Consolation were diminished within him, and he no longer felt that joy which he had formerly in the cleansing of the stables, in the washing of the dishes, and in the sweeping of the holy places, from which he was now relieved by reason of bodily weakness. He was tormented with the fear that his penances might not sufficiently atone for the sinful pleasures of his past life, of which he had a vivid and growing remembrance. The thought was ever present with him that he might not be predestined to die in the odour of sanctity.

In this anguish of heart he went forth one day into the wood which lies on the top of the mountain of La Verna, beyond the Friary, and ran up and down, stumbling among the roots of the trees and calling aloud with sighs and tears, "Little wretch, thou art lost! Abominable sinner Angelo, how shalt thou find a holy death?"

To him, in this distraction, comes the Warden with three of the elder friars and asks him what has befallen him.

"The fear of dying in my sins," cries Angelo.

"You have the comfort of the Gospel, my son," says the Warden.

"It is not enough for me," sobs Angelo, beating his wounded breast. "You know not how great were my pleasures in the world!"

With that he starts away again to wander through the wood, but the Warden restrains him, and soothes him, and speaks comfortably to him; and at last Angelo makes his request that he may have a certain cave in the woods for his dwelling and be enclosed there as a recluse to await the coming of a holy death.

"But, my son," objects the Warden, "what will the Friary do without the example of your devotion and your service?"

"I will pray for you all," says Angelo; "night and day I will give myself to intercession for the order of friars minor."

So the Warden consents, and Angelo, for the time, is satisfied.

Now, the top of the mountain of La Verna is full of rude clefts and caverns, with broken and jagged rocks. Truly, it were a frightful place to behold but for the tall trees that have grown up among the rocks, clasping them with their roots, and the trailing vines and gentle wild flowers and green ferns that spring abundantly around them as if in token of kindness and good-will and bounty.

All these were much beloved of St. Francis, who heard every creature cry aloud, saying "God made me for thee, O man." So great was his affection for them that he would not have his little friars cut down a whole tree for firewood, but bade them only lop the branches and let the tree live in joy. And he taught them to make no garden of pot-herbs only, but to leave room always for the flowers, for love of One who was called "the rose of Sharon," and "the lily of the valley."

But this was not the mind of Angelo, who stumbled to his reclusery blindly, intent only on the thought of his death, and never marking the fine lace-work of the ferns that were broken by his passing nor the sweet fragrance of the flowers crushed beneath his feet.

The cave which he had chosen lay a little beyond that most sacred cavern where St. Francis had fasted and where the falcon had visited him every morning, beating her wings and singing to rouse him softly to matins, and where at last he had received in his body the marks of the Holy Cross.

It was on the side of the mountain looking toward the west, and in front of it was a narrow, deep, and terrible chasm, which could only be crossed by a log laid in the manner of a bridge. But the cave itself looked out beyond into the wide and fruitful Val d'Arno, with the stream of silver coiling through it, and on the other side the wooded mountains of Valombrosa and Pratomagno.

Of this Angelo saw nothing, as he passed by the log bridge into the cave. The three friars who went with him walled up the entrance with stones, except for an opening at the height of a man's breast; and they returned, taking away the log at his request and casting it down the cliff. After that the food of Angelo was thrown across the chasm into the opening of the cave, and to drink he had a small spring of water trickling among the rocks a drop at a time, and he lived as a recluse considering only how to make a saintly end.

His thoughts were thus fixed and centred upon his own great concern, to a degree that made the world turn to nothing around him. Even the Friary seemed to lie at an infinite distance, and the prayers which he had promised to offer for it were more in word than in desire. There was no warmth in them, for all the fire of his soul had burned into one thought which consumed him. Day and night he cried, "O wicked life, let me go into a holy death!"

But he came no nearer to his goal, nor could he find any assurance that he was elect and chosen to attain it. On the contrary his anxiety increased and misery became his companion. For this reason: in his dreams he dwelt continually upon the most sinful pleasures of his past life, and they grew upon him; but in his waking hours he considered and measured the greatness of his penances, yet without ever arriving at the certainty that they balanced his offences.

Now, you are not to suppose that the past life of Angelo, though vain and worldly and streaked with evil, had been altogether woven of black threads. For he had been of an open and kindly heart, ready to share with others in the joy of living, greatly pleased to do a good turn to his neighbours, compassionate and gentle-natured, a lover of music and of little children. So there were many things in his youth of which he had no need to be ashamed, since they were both innocent and merry, and the white and golden threads of a pure and grateful happiness were not wanting in the fabric of his loom.

But of these he would not think, being set upon recalling only the sinful hours that needed repentance. And of these he thought so constantly that in the visions of the night they lived again, twining their limbs about him and pressing their burning lips upon his. But when he awoke he was filled with terror, and fell to counting the severities and privations which he had endured for an atonement. So it came to pass that he was strangely and dreadfully merry dreaming, but strangely and desperately sad waking. And between the two he found no peace, nor ever escaped from the trouble and anguish of himself.

After a twelvemonth or more of this life, very early in the morning he awoke from a hot dream with horror, and groaned aloud, "If I die, I am damned."

"How so, little sheep of God," said a voice near at hand; "who has led thee into the wilderness?"

Fra Angelo lifted his head and looked at the opening of the cave, but there was no one there. Then he looked behind him, and on both sides, but he saw no one. Yet so clear and certain was the sound of the voice that he could not rest, but went to the entrance and thrust out his head.

On the shelf of the rock in front of the cave he saw a short and spare brother dressed in the habit of a friar minor, with a thin black beard, and dark simple eyes, kindled with gentle flames. In his right hand he held a stick of wood, as it were the bow of a viol, and this he drew across his left arm, singing the while in French a hymn of joy for the sun, his brother, and for the wind, his companion, and for the water, his sister, and for the earth, his mother.

At this Fra Angelo was astonished and confused, for these songs had not been heard in the Friary since many years, and it seemed as if some foreign brother must have come from France with strange customs. But when he looked more closely he saw that the long and delicate hands of the little brother were pierced in the palm, and his feet were wounded as if a nail had passed through them. Then he knew that he saw St. Francis, and he was so ashamed and afraid that he clung to the rocks and could not speak.

Then the little brother turned from looking out upon the morning in Val d'Arno and looked at Fra Angelo. After a long while he said, very softly, "What doest thou here in the cave, dearest?"

"Blessed father," stammered the recluse, "I dwell in solitude, to atone for my worldly life and find a holy death."

"That is for thyself," said the little brother in the sun; "but for others what doest thou?"

Angelo thought a moment and answered, humbly, "I give them an ensample of holiness."

"They need more," said the little brother smiling, "and thou must give it."

"Blessed father," cried Angelo, "command me and I will obey thee, for thou art in heaven and I am near to hell."

"Listen, then, thou lost sheep," said the little brother, "and I will show thee the way. Climb over the wall. Lay aside the breastplate and rings of iron—they hinder thee. Come near and sit beside me. In a certain city there is a poor widow whose child is sick even unto death. Go unto her with this box of electuary, and give it to the child that he may recover. I command thee by Obedience."

So saying he laid in the hand of Angelo a box of olive-wood, filled with an electuary so sweet that the fragrance of it went through the wood. But Angelo was confused.

"How shall I know the way," said he, "when I know not the city?"

"Stand up," answered the little brother with the wounded hands, "and close thine eyes firmly. Now turn round and round as children do, until I bid thee stop."

So Fra Angelo, fearing a little because the shelf of rock was narrow, shut tight his eyes and, stretching out his arms, turned round and round until he was dizzy. Then he fell to the ground, and when he looked up the little brother of the sun was gone.

But the head of Fra Angelo lay toward the city of Poppi on the other side of the valley, so he knew that this was the way, and he went down from the mountain.

As he went, his bodily weakness departed and the pains of his worn flesh left him, and he rejoiced in the brightness of the world. The linnets and blackbirds that sang in the thickets were the children of those that had been brothers of the air to St. Francis, and the larks that bubbled up from the fields wore the same sad-coloured garments and chanted the same joyous music that he had commended. The primroses and the violets and the cyclamens had not forgotten to bloom because of sin, and the pure incense of their breath went forth unto gladness.

So Fra Angelo made his journey with a light heart, quickly, and came to the city of Poppi. There he found the poor widow with her child sick unto death, and he gave them the olive-wood box. The child took the electuary eagerly, for it was pleasant to the taste, and it did him good more than if it had been bitter. So presently the fever left him, and the mother rejoiced and blessed St. Francis and Fra Angelo. And he said, "I must be going."

Now, as he went and returned toward La Verna, he passed through a village, and in the field at the side of it he saw many children quarrelling.

"Why do you fight," said Angelo, laying hands on two of them, "when you might be playing?"

"Because we know not what to play," they answered; and some shouted one thing and some another.

"Let the older ones play at Fox and Geese," said Angelo; "and look, here is a plank! We will put it over this great stone and I will play at seesaw with the little ones."

Then the children all laughed when they saw a friar playing at seesaw; but he went up and down merrily, and they were all glad together. After a while they grew weary of the games, and Angelo asked what they would do next.

"Dance," cried the children; "dance and sing!"

"But where is the music?" said Angelo.

So one of the boys ran away to a house in the village and came back presently with an old viol and a bow. Angelo fingered the instrument, and tuned it, for he had been a skilful musician.

"Now I will teach you," said he, "a very sweet music that I heard this morning. And do you all sing as I teach you, and between the songs take hands and dance around."

Then he sat down upon a grassy hillock, with the children in a circle about him, and he taught them the songs that were sung by the little brother of the sun and of the wind and of the water and of the birds—even by that minstrel of God who came to the cave with the morning light. Between the verses the children, holding hands, danced in a ring around Fra Angelo, while he played upon the old viol.

As he played thus, he was aware of a hand upon his shoulder, and supposed it to be one of the children.

"Go back," he said, "go back to your place, dearest naughty one; the song is not finished."

"It is finished," said a voice behind him. "This is the right ending of the song."

And Angelo, looking up in amazement, saw the face of an angel, and the bow dropped from his fingers.

When the music ceased, the children broke their ring and ran to Angelo where he lay upon the grass. They wondered to see him so still and pale, yet because his face was smiling they were not afraid.

"He is weary," they cried; "the good friar has fallen asleep—perhaps he has fainted. Let us run and call help for him."

But they did not understand that the messenger of Holy Death had passed among them and called Angelo in the odour of sanctity.

THE SAD SHEPHERD

I

DARKNESS

Out of the Valley of Gardens, where a film of new-fallen snow lay smooth as feathers on the breast of a dove, the ancient Pools of Solomon looked up into the night sky with dark, tranquil eyes, wide-open and passive, reflecting the crisp stars and the small, round moon. The full springs, overflowing on the hillside, melted their way through the field of white in winding channels, and along their course the grass was green even in the dead of winter.

But the sad shepherd walked far above the friendly valley, in a region where ridges of gray rock welted and scarred the back of the earth, like wounds of half-forgotten strife and battles long ago. The solitude was forbidding and disquieting; the keen air that searched the wanderer had no pity in it; and the myriad glances of the night were curiously cold.

His flock straggled after him. The sheep, weather beaten and dejected, followed the path with low heads nodding from side to side, as if they had travelled far and found little pasture. The black, lop-eared goats leaped upon the rocks, restless and ravenous, tearing down the tender branches and leaves of the dwarf oaks and wild olives. They reared up against the twisted trunks and crawled and scrambled among the boughs. It was like a company of gray downcast friends and a troop of merry little black devils following the sad shepherd afar off.

He walked looking on the ground, paying small heed to them. Now and again, when the sound of pattering feet and panting breath and the rustling and rending among the copses fell too far behind, he drew out his shepherd's pipe and blew a strain of music, shrill and plaintive, quavering and lamenting through the hollow night. He waited while the troops of gray and black scuffled and bounded and trotted near to him. Then he dropped the pipe into its place again and strode forward, looking on the ground.

The fitful, shivery wind that rasped the hill-top, fluttered the rags of his long mantle of Tyrian blue, torn by thorns and stained by travel. The rich tunic of striped silk beneath it was worn thin, and the girdle about his loins had lost all its ornaments of silver and jewels. His curling hair hung down dishevelled under a turban of fine linen, in which the gilt threads were frayed and tarnished; and his shoes of soft leather were broken by the road. On his brown fingers the places of the vanished rings were still marked in white skin. He carried not the long staff nor the heavy nail-studded rod of the shepherd, but a slender stick of carved cedar battered and scratched by hard usage, and the handle, which must once have been of precious metal, was missing.

He was a strange figure for that lonely place and that humble occupation—a branch of faded beauty from some royal garden tossed by rude winds into the wilderness—a pleasure craft adrift, buffeted and broken, on rough seas.

But he seemed to have passed beyond caring. His young face was as frayed and threadbare as his garments. The splendour of the moonlight flooding the wild world meant as little to him as the hardness of the rugged track which he followed. He wrapped his tattered mantle closer around him, and strode ahead, looking on the ground.

As the path dropped from the summit of the ridge toward the Valley of Mills and passed among huge broken rocks, three men sprang at him from the shadows. He lifted his stick, but let it fall again, and a strange ghost of a smile twisted his face as they gripped him and threw him down.

"You are rough beggars," he said. "Say what you want, you are welcome to it."

"Your money, dog of a courtier," they muttered fiercely; "give us your golden collar, Herod's hound, quick, or you die!"

"The quicker the better," he answered, closing his eyes.

The bewildered flock of sheep and goats, gathered in a silent ring, stood at gaze while the robbers fumbled over their master.

"This is a stray dog," said one, "he has lost his collar, there is not even the price of a mouthful of wine on him. Shall we kill him and leave him for the vultures?"

"What have the vultures done for us," said another, "that we should feed them? Let us take his cloak and drive off his flock, and leave him to die in his own time."

With a kick and a curse they left him. He opened his eyes and lay quiet for a moment, with his twisted smile, watching the stars.

"You creep like snails," he said. "I thought you had marked my time to-night. But not even that is given to me for nothing. I must pay for all, it seems."

Far away, slowly scattering and receding, he heard the rustling and bleating of his frightened flock as the robbers, running and shouting, tried to drive them over the hills. Then he stood up and took the shepherd's pipe from the breast of his tunic. He blew again that plaintive, piercing air, sounding it out over the ridges and distant thickets. It seemed to have neither beginning nor end; a melancholy, pleading tune that searched forever after something lost.

While he played, the sheep and the goats, slipping away from their captors by roundabout ways, hiding behind the laurel bushes, following the dark gullies, leaping down the broken cliffs, came circling back to him, one after another; and as they came, he interrupted his playing, now and then, to call them by name.

When they were nearly all assembled, he went down swiftly toward the lower valley, and they followed him, panting. At the last crook of the path on the steep hillside a straggler came after him along the cliff. He looked up and saw it outlined against the sky. Then he saw it leap, and slip, and fall beyond the path into a deep cleft.

"Little fool," he said, "fortune is kind to you! You have escaped from the big trap of life. What? You are crying for help? You are still in the trap? Then I must go down to you, little fool, for I am a fool too. But why I must do it, I know no more than you know."

He lowered himself quickly and perilously into the cleft, and found the creature with its leg broken and bleeding. It was not a sheep but a young goat. He had no cloak to wrap it in, but he took off his turban and unrolled it, and bound it around the trembling animal. Then he climbed back to the path and strode on at the head of his flock, carrying the little black kid in his arms.

There were houses in the Valley of the Mills; and in some of them lights were burning; and the drone of the mill-stones, where the women were still grinding, came out into the night like the humming of drowsy bees. As the women heard the pattering and bleating of the flock, they wondered who was passing so late. One of them, in a house where there was no mill but many lights, came to the door and looked out laughing, her face and bosom bare.

But the sad shepherd did not stay. His long shadow and the confused mass of lesser shadows behind him drifted down the white moonlight, past the yellow bars of lamplight that gleamed from the doorways. It seemed as if he were bound to go somewhere and would not delay.

Yet with all his haste to be gone, it was plain that he thought little of where he was going. For when he came to the foot of the valley, where the paths divided, he stood between them staring vacantly, without a desire to turn him this way or that. The imperative of choice halted him like a barrier. The balance of his mind hung even because both scales were empty. He could act, he could go, for his strength was untouched; but he could not choose, for his will was broken within him.

The path to the left went up toward the little town of Bethlehem, with huddled roofs and walls in silhouette along the double-crested hill. It was dark and forbidding as a closed fortress. The sad shepherd looked at it with indifferent eyes; there was nothing there to draw him.

The path to the right wound through rock-strewn valleys toward the Dead Sea. But rising out of that crumpled wilderness, a mile or two away, the smooth white ribbon of a chariot-road lay upon the flank of a cone-shaped mountain and curled in loops toward its peak. There the great cone was cut squarely off, and the levelled summit was capped by a palace of marble, with round towers at the corners and flaring beacons along the walls; and the glow of an immense fire, hidden in the central court-yard, painted a false dawn in the eastern sky. All down the clean-cut mountain slopes, on terraces and blind arcades, the lights flashed from lesser pavilions and pleasure-houses.

It was the secret orchard of Herod and his friends, their trysting-place with the spirits of mirth and madness. They called it the Mountain of the Little Paradise. Rich gardens were there; and the cool water from the Pools of Solomon plashed in the fountains; and trees of the knowledge of good and evil fruited blood-red and ivory-white above them; and smooth, curving, glistening shapes, whispering softly of pleasure, lay among the flowers and glided behind the trees. All this was now hidden in the dark. Only the strange bulk of the mountain, a sharp black pyramid girdled and crowned with fire, loomed across the night—a mountain once seen never to be forgotten.

The sad shepherd remembered it well. He looked at it with the eyes of a child who has been in hell. It burned him from afar. Turning neither to the right nor to the left, he walked without a path straight out upon the plain of Bethlehem, still whitened in the hollows and on the sheltered side of its rounded hillocks by the veil of snow.

He faced a wide and empty world. To the west in sleeping Bethlehem, to the east in flaring Herodium, the life of man was infinitely far away from him. Even the stars seemed to withdraw themselves against the blue-black of the sky. They diminished and receded till they were like pin-holes in the vault above him. The moon in mid-heaven shrank into a bit of burnished silver, hard and glittering, immeasurably remote. The ragged, inhospitable ridges of Tekoa lay stretched in mortal slumber along the horizon, and between them he caught a glimpse of the sunken Lake of Death, darkly gleaming in its deep bed. There was no movement, no sound, on the plain where he walked, except the soft-padding feet of his dumb, obsequious flock.

He felt an endless isolation strike cold to his heart, against which he held the limp body of the wounded kid, wondering the while, with a half-contempt for his own foolishness, why he took such trouble to save a tiny scrap of the worthless tissue which is called life.

Even when a man does not know or care where he is going, if he steps onward he will get there. In an hour or more of walking over the plain the sad shepherd came to a sheepfold of grey stones with a rude tower beside it. The fold was full of sheep, and at the foot of the tower a little fire of thorns was burning, around which four shepherds were crouching, wrapped in their thick woollen cloaks.

As the stranger approached they looked up, and one of them rose quickly to his feet, grasping his knotted club. But when they saw the flock that followed the sad shepherd, they stared at each other and said: "It is one of us, a keeper of sheep. But how comes he here in this raiment? It is what men wear in kings' houses."

"No," said the one who was standing, "it is what they wear when they have been thrown out of them. Look at the rags. He may be a thief and a robber with his stolen flock."

"Salute him when he comes near," said the oldest shepherd. "Are we not four to one? We have nothing to fear from a ragged traveller. Speak him fair. It is the will of God—and it costs nothing."

"Peace be with you, brother," cried the youngest shepherd; "may your mother and father be blessed."

"May your heart be enlarged," the stranger answered, "and may all your families be more blessed than mine, for I have none."

"A homeless man," said the old shepherd, "has either been robbed by his fellows, or punished by God."

"I do not know which it was," answered the stranger; "the end is the same, as you see."

"By your speech you come from Galilee. Where are you going? What are you seeking here?"

"I was going nowhere, my masters; but it was cold on the way there, and my feet turned to your fire."

"Come then, if you are a peaceable man, and warm your feet with us. Heat is a good gift; divide it and it is not less. But you shall have bread and salt too, if you will."

"May your hospitality enrich you. I am your unworthy guest. But my flock?"

"Let your flock shelter by the south wall of the fold: there is good picking there and no wind. Come you and sit with us."

So they all sat down by the fire; and the sad shepherd ate of their bread, but sparingly, like a man to whom hunger brings a need but no joy in the satisfying of it; and the others were silent for a proper time, out of courtesy. Then the oldest shepherd spoke:

"My name is Zadok the son of Eliezer, of Bethlehem. I am the chief shepherd of the flocks of the Temple, which are before you in the fold. These are my sister's sons, Jotham, and Shama, and Nathan: their father Elkanah is dead; and but for these I am a childless man."

"My name," replied the stranger, "is Ammiel the son of Jochanan, of the city of Bethsaida, by the Sea of Galilee, and I am a fatherless man."

"It is better to be childless than fatherless," said Zadok, "yet it is the will of God that children should bury their fathers. When did the blessed Jochanan die?"

"I know not whether he be dead or alive. It is three years since I looked upon his face or had word of him."

"You are an exile, then? he has cast you off?"

"It was the other way," said Ammiel, looking on the ground.

At this the shepherd Shama, who had listened with doubt in his face, started up in anger. "Pig of a Galilean," he cried, "despiser of parents! breaker of the law! When I saw you coming I knew you for something vile. Why do you darken the night for us with your presence? You have reviled him who begot you. Away, or we stone you!"

Ammiel did not answer or move. The twisted smile passed over his face again as he waited to know the shepherds' will with him, even as he had waited for the robbers. But Zadok lifted his hand.

"Not so hasty, Shama-ben-Elkanah. You also break the law by judging a man unheard. The rabbis have told us that there is a tradition of the elders—a rule as holy as the law itself—that a man may deny his father in a certain way without sin. It is a strange rule, and it must be very holy or it would not be so strange. But this is the teaching of the elders: a son may say of anything for which his father asks him—a sheep, or a measure of corn, or a field, or a purse of silver—'it is Corban, a gift that I have vowed unto the Lord'; and so his father shall have no more claim upon him. Have you said 'Corban' to your father, Ammiel-ben-Jochanan? Have you made a vow unto the Lord?"

"I have said 'Corban,'" answered Ammiel, lifting his face, still shadowed by that strange smile, "but it was not the Lord who heard my vow."

"Tell us what you have done," said the old man sternly, "for we will neither judge you, nor shelter you, unless we hear your story."

"There is nothing in it," replied Ammiel indifferently. "It is an old story. But if you are curious you shall hear it. Afterward you shall deal with me as you will."

So the shepherds, wrapped in their warm cloaks, sat listening with grave faces and watchful, unsearchable eyes, while Ammiel in his tattered silk sat by the sinking fire of thorns and told his tale with a voice that had no room for hope or fear—a cool, dead voice that spoke only of things ended.

II

NIGHTFIRE

"In my father's house I was the second son. My brother was honoured and trusted in all things. He was a prudent man and profitable to the house-hold. All that he counselled was done, all that he wished he had. My place was a narrow one. There was neither honour nor joy in it, for it was filled with daily tasks and rebukes. No one cared for me. My mother sometimes wept when I was rebuked. Perhaps she was disappointed in me. But she had no power to make things better. I felt that I was a beast of burden, fed only in order that I might be useful; and the dull life irked me like an ill-fitting harness. There was nothing in it.

"I went to my father and claimed my share of the inheritance. He was rich. He gave it to me. It did not impoverish him and it made me free. I said to him 'Corban,' and shook the dust of Bethsaida from my feet.

"I went out to look for mirth and love and joy and all that is pleasant to the eyes and sweet to the taste. If a god made me, thought I, he made me to live, and the pride of life was strong in my heart and in my flesh. My vow was offered to that well-known god. I served him in Jerusalem, in Alexandria, in Rome, for his altars are everywhere and men worship him openly or in secret.

"My money and youth made me welcome to his followers, and I spent them both freely as if they could never come to an end. I clothed myself in purple and fine linen and fared sumptuously every day. The wine of Cyprus and the dishes of Egypt and Syria were on my table. My dwelling was crowded with merry guests. They came for what I gave them. Their faces were hungry and their soft touch was like the clinging of leeches. To them I was nothing but money and youth; no longer a beast of burden—a beast of pleasure. There was nothing in it.

"From the richest fare my heart went away empty, and after the wildest banquet my soul fell drunk and solitary into sleep.

"Then I thought, Power is better than pleasure. If a man will feast and revel let him do it with the great. They will favour him and raise him up for the service that he renders them. He will obtain place and authority in the world and gain many friends. So I joined myself to Herod."

When the sad shepherd spoke this name his listeners drew back from him as if it were a defilement to hear it. They spat upon the ground and cursed the Idumean who called himself their king.

"A slave!" Jotham cried, "a bloody tyrant and a slave from Edom! A fox, a vile beast who devours his own children! God burn him in Gehenna."

The old Zadok picked up a stone and threw it into the darkness, saying slowly, "I cast this stone on the grave of the Idumean, the blasphemer, the defiler of the Temple! God send us soon the Deliverer, the Promised One, the true King of Israel!" Ammiel made no sign, but went on with his story.

"Herod used me well—for his own purpose. He welcomed me to his palace and his table, and gave me a place among his favourites. He was so much my friend that he borrowed my money. There were many of the nobles of Jerusalem with him, Sadducees, and proselytes from Rome and Asia, and women from everywhere. The law of Israel was observed in the open court, when the people were watching. But in the secret feasts there was no law but the will of Herod, and many deities were served but no god was worshipped. There the captains and the princes of Rome consorted with the high-priest and his sons by night; and there was much coming and going by hidden ways. Everybody was a borrower or a lender, a buyer or a seller of favours. It was a house of diligent madness. There was nothing in it.

"In the midst of this whirling life a great need of love came upon me and I wished to hold some one in my inmost heart.

"At a certain place in the city, within closed doors, I saw a young slave-girl dancing. She was about fifteen years old, thin and supple; she danced like a reed in the wind; but her eyes were weary as death, and her white body was marked with bruises. She stumbled, and the men laughed at her. She fell, and her mistress beat her, crying out that she would fain be rid of such a heavy-footed slave. I paid the price and took her to my dwelling.

"Her name was Tamar. She was a daughter of Lebanon. I robed her in silk and broidered linen. I nourished her with tender care so that beauty came upon her like the blossoming of an almond tree; she was a garden enclosed, breathing spices. Her eyes were like doves behind her veil, her lips were a thread of scarlet, her neck was a tower of ivory, and her breasts were as two fawns which feed among the lilies. She was whiter than milk, and more rosy than the flower of the peach, and her dancing was like the flight of a bird among the branches. So I loved her.

"She lay in my bosom as a clear stone that one has bought and polished and set in fine gold at the end of a golden chain. Never was she glad at my coming, or sorry at my going. Never did she give me anything except what I took from her. There was nothing in it.

"Now whether Herod knew of the jewel that I kept in my dwelling I cannot tell. It was sure that he had his spies in all the city, and himself walked the streets by night in a disguise. On a certain day he sent for me, and had me into his secret chamber, professing great love toward me and more confidence than in any man that lived. So I must go to Rome for him, bearing a sealed letter and a private message to Cæsar. All my goods would be left safely in the hands of the king, my friend, who would reward me double. There was a certain place of high authority at Jerusalem which Cæsar would gladly bestow on a Jew who had done him a service. This mission would commend me to him. It was a great occasion, suited to my powers. Thus Herod fed me with fair promises, and I ran his errand. There was nothing in it.

"I stood before Cæsar and gave him the letter. He read it and laughed, saying that a prince with an incurable hunger is a servant of value to an emperor. Then he asked me if there was nothing sent with the letter. I answered that there was no gift, but a message for his private ear. He drew me aside and I told him that Herod begged earnestly that his dear son, Antipater, might be sent back in haste from Rome to Palestine, for the king had great need of him.

"At this Cæsar laughed again. 'To bury him, I suppose,' said he, 'with his brothers, Alexander and Aristobulus! Truly, it is better to be Herod's swine than his son! Tell the old fox he may catch his own prey.' With this he turned from me and I withdrew unrewarded, to make my way back, as best I could with an empty purse, to Palestine. I had seen the Lord of the World. There was nothing in it.

"Selling my rings and bracelets I got passage in a trading ship for Joppa. There I heard that the king was not in Jerusalem, at his Palace of the Upper City, but had gone with his friends to make merry for a month on the Mountain of the Little Paradise. On that hill-top over against us, where the lights are flaring to-night, in the banquet-hall where couches are spread for a hundred guests, I found Herod."

The listening shepherds spat upon the ground again, and Jotham muttered, "May the worms that devour his flesh never die!" But Zadok whispered, "We wait for the Lord's salvation to come out of Zion." And the sad shepherd, looking with fixed eyes at the firelit mountain far away, continued his story:

"The king lay on his ivory couch, and the sweat of his disease was heavy upon him, for he was old, and his flesh was corrupted. But his hair and his beard were dyed and perfumed and there was a wreath of roses on his head. The hall was full of nobles and great men, the sons of the high-priest were there, and the servants poured their wine in cups of gold. There was a sound of soft music; and all the men were watching a girl who danced in the middle of the hall; and the eyes of Herod were fiery, like the eyes of a fox.

"The dancer was Tamar. She glistened like the snow on Lebanon, and the redness of her was ruddier than a pomegranate, and her dancing was like the coiling of white serpents. When the dance was ended her attendants threw a veil of gauze over her and she lay among her cushions, half covered with flowers, at the feet of the king.

"Through the sound of clapping hands and shouting, two slaves led me behind the couch of Herod. His eyes narrowed as they fell upon me. I told him the message of Cæsar, making it soft, as if it were a word that suffered him to catch his prey. He stroked his beard and his look fell on Tamar. 'I have caught it,' he murmured; 'by all the gods, I have always caught it. And my dear son, Antipater, is coming home of his own will. I have lured him, he is mine.'

"Then a look of madness crossed his face and he sprang up, with frothing lips, and struck at me. 'What is this,' he cried, 'a spy, a servant of my false son, a traitor in my banquet-hall! Who are you?' I knelt before him, protesting that he must know me; that I was his friend, his messenger; that I had left all my goods in his hands; that the girl who had danced for him was mine. At this his face changed again and he fell back on his couch, shaken with horrible laughter. 'Yours!' he cried, 'when was she yours? What is yours? I know you now, poor madman. You are Ammiel, a crazy shepherd from Galilee, who troubled us some time since. Take him away, slaves. He has twenty sheep and twenty goats among my flocks at the foot of the mountain. See to it that he gets them, and drive him away.'

"I fought against the slaves with my bare hands, but they held me. I called to Tamar, begging her to have pity on me, to speak for me, to come with me. She looked up with her eyes like doves behind her veil, but there was no knowledge of me in them. She laughed lazily, as if it were a poor comedy, and flung a broken rose-branch in my face. Then the silver cord was loosened within me, and my heart went out, and I struggled no more. There was nothing in it.

"Afterward I found myself on the road with this flock. I led them past Hebron into the south country, and so by the Vale of Eshcol, and over many hills beyond the Pools of Solomon, until my feet brought me to your fire. Here I rest on the way to nowhere."

He sat silent, and the four shepherds looked at him with amazement.

"It is a bitter tale," said Shama, "and you are a great sinner."

"I should be a fool not to know that," answered the sad shepherd, "but the knowledge does me no good."

"You must repent," said Nathan, the youngest shepherd, in a friendly voice.

"How can a man repent," answered the sad shepherd, "unless he has hope? But I am sorry for everything, and most of all for living."

"Would you not live to kill the fox Herod?" cried Jotham fiercely.

"Why should I let him out of the trap," answered the sad shepherd. "Is he not dying more slowly than I could kill him?"

"You must have faith in God," said Zadok earnestly and gravely.

"He is too far away."

"Then you must have love for your neighbour."

"He is too near. My confidence in man was like a pool by the wayside. It was shallow, but there was water in it, and sometimes a star shone there. Now the feet of many beasts have trampled through it, and the jackals have drunken of it, and there is no more water. It is dry and the mire is caked at the bottom."

"Is there nothing good in the world?"

"There is pleasure, but I am sick of it. There is power, but I hate it. There is wisdom, but I mistrust it. Life is a game and every player is for his own hand. Mine is played. I have nothing to win or lose."

"You are young, you have many years to live."

"I am old, yet the days before me are too many."

"But you travel the road, you go forward. Do you hope for nothing?"

"I hope for nothing," said the sad shepherd. "Yet if one thing should come to me it might be the beginning of hope. If I saw in man or woman a deed of kindness without a selfish reason, and a proof of love gladly given for its own sake only, then might I turn my face toward that light. Till that comes, how can I have faith in God whom I have never seen? I have seen the world which he has made, and it brings me no faith. There is nothing in it."

"Ammiel-ben-Jochanan," said the old man sternly, "you are a son of Israel, and we have had compassion on you, according to the law. But you are an apostate, an unbeliever, and we can have no more fellowship with you, lest a curse come upon us. The company of the desperate brings misfortune. Go your way and depart from us, for our way is not yours."

So the sad shepherd thanked them for their entertainment, and took the little kid again in his arms, and went into the night, calling his flock. But the youngest shepherd Nathan followed him a few steps and said:

"There is a broken fold at the foot of the hill. It is old and small, but you may find a shelter there for your flock where the wind will not shake you. Go your way with God, brother, and see better days."

Then Ammiel went a little way down the hill and sheltered his flock in a corner of the crumbling walls. He lay among the sheep and the goats with his face upon his folded arms, and whether the time passed slowly or swiftly he did not know, for he slept.

He waked as Nathan came running and stumbling among the scattered stones.

"We have seen a vision," he cried, "a wonderful vision of angels. Did you not hear them? They sang loudly of the Hope of Israel. We are going to Bethlehem to see this thing which is come to pass. Come you and keep watch over our sheep while we are gone."

"Of angels I have seen and heard nothing," said Ammiel, "but I will guard your flocks with mine, since I am in debt to you for bread and fire."

So he brought the kid in his arms, and the weary flock straggling after him, to the south wall of the great fold again, and sat there by the embers at the foot of the tower, while the others were away.

The moon rested like a ball on the edge of the western hills and rolled behind them. The stars faded in the east and the fires went out on the Mountain of the Little Paradise. Over the hills of Moab a gray flood of dawn rose slowly, and arrows of red shot far up before the sunrise.

The shepherds returned full of joy and told what they had seen.

"It was even as the angels said unto us," said Shama, "and it must be true. The King of Israel has come. The faithful shall be blessed."

"Herod shall fall," cried Jotham, lifting his clenched fist toward the dark peaked mountain. "Burn, black Idumean, in the bottomless pit, where the fire is not quenched."

Zadok spoke more quietly. "We found the new-born child of whom the angels told us wrapped in swaddling clothes and lying in a manger. The ways of God are wonderful. His salvation comes out of darkness. But you, Ammiel-ben-Jochanan, except you believe, you shall not see it. Yet since you have kept our flocks faithfully, and because of the joy that has come to us, I give you this piece of silver to help you on your way."

But Nathan came close to the sad shepherd and touched him on the shoulder with a friendly hand. "Go you also to Bethlehem," he said in a low voice, "for it is good to see what we have seen, and we will keep your flock until you return."

"I will go," said Ammiel, looking into his face, "for I think you wish me well. But whether I shall see what you have seen, or whether I shall ever return, I know not. Farewell."

III

DAWN

The narrow streets of Bethlehem were waking to the first stir of life as the sad shepherd came into the town with the morning, and passed through them like one walking in his sleep.

The court-yard of the great khan and the open rooms around it were crowded with travellers, rousing from their night's rest and making ready for the day's journey. In front of the stables half hollowed in the rock beside the inn, men were saddling their horses and their beasts of burden, and there was much noise and confusion.

But beyond these, at the end of the line, there was a deeper grotto in the rock, which was used only when the nearer stalls were full. Beside the entrance of this cave an ass was tethered, and a man of middle age stood in the doorway.

The sad shepherd saluted him and told his name.

"I am Joseph the carpenter of Nazareth," replied the man. "Have you also seen the angels of whom your brother shepherds came to tell us?"

"I have seen no angels," answered Ammiel, "nor have I any brothers among the shepherds. But I would fain see what they have seen."

"It is our first-born son," said Joseph, "and the Most High has sent him to us. He is a marvellous child: great things are foretold of him. You may go in, but quietly, for the child and his mother Mary are asleep."

So the sad shepherd went in quietly. His long shadow entered before him, for the sunrise was flowing into the door of the grotto. It was made clean and put in order, and a bed of straw was laid in the corner on the ground.

The child was asleep, but the young mother was waking, for she had taken him from the manger into her lap, where her maiden veil of white was spread to receive him. And she was singing very softly as she bent over him in wonder and content.

Ammiel saluted her and kneeled down to look at the child. He saw nothing different from other young children. The mother waited for him to speak of angels, as the other shepherds had done. The sad shepherd did not speak, but only looked And as he looked his face changed.

"You have suffered pain and danger and sorrow for his sake," he said gently.

"They are past," she answered, "and for his sake I have suffered them gladly."

"He is very little and helpless; you must bear many troubles for his sake."

"To care for him is my joy, and to bear him lightens my burden."

"He does not know you, he can do nothing for you."

"But I know him. I have carried him under my heart, he is my son and my king."

"Why do you love him?"

The mother looked up at the sad shepherd with a great reproach in her soft eyes. Then her look grew pitiful as it rested on his face.

"You are a sorrowful man," she said.

"I am a wicked man," he answered.

She shook her head gently.

"I know nothing of that," she said, "but you must be very sorrowful, since you are born of a woman and yet you ask a mother why she loves her child. I love him for love's sake, because God has given him to me."

So the mother Mary leaned over her little son again and began to croon a song as if she were alone with him.

But Ammiel was still there, watching and thinking and beginning to remember. It came back to him that there was a woman in Galilee who had wept when he was rebuked; whose eyes had followed him when he was unhappy, as if she longed to do something for him; whose voice had broken and dropped silent while she covered her tear-stained face when he went away.

His thoughts flowed swiftly and silently toward her and after her like rapid waves of light. There was a thought of her bending over a little child in her lap, singing softly for pure joy,—and the child was himself. There was a thought of her lifting a little child to the breast that had borne him as a burden and a pain, to nourish him there as a comfort and a treasure,—and the child was himself. There was a thought of her watching and tending and guiding a little child from day to day, from year to year, putting tender arms around him, bending over his first wavering steps, rejoicing in his joys, wiping away the tears from his eyes, as he had never tried to wipe her tears away,—and the child was himself. She had done everything for the child's sake, but what had the child done for her sake? And the child was himself: that was what he had come to,—after the nightfire had burned out, after the darkness had grown thin and melted in the thoughts that pulsed through it like rapid waves of light,—that was what he had come to in the early morning,—*himself*, a child in his mother's arms.

Then he arose and went out of the grotto softly, making the three-fold sign of reverence; and the eyes of Mary followed him with kind looks.

Joseph of Nazareth was still waiting outside the door.

"How was it that you did not see the angels?" he asked. "Were you not with the other shepherds?"

"No," answered Ammiel, "I was asleep. But I have seen the mother and the child. Blessed be the house that holds them."

"You are strangely clad for a shepherd," said Joseph. "Where do you come from?"

"From a far country," replied Ammiel; "from a country that you have never visited."

"Where are you going now?" asked Joseph.

"I am going home," answered Ammiel, "to my mother's and my father's house in Galilee."

"Go in peace, friend," said Joseph.

And the sad shepherd took up his battered staff, and went on his way rejoicing.

THE MANSION

I

There was an air of calm and reserved opulence about the Weightman mansion that spoke not of money squandered, but of wealth prudently applied. Standing on a corner of the Avenue no longer fashionable for residence, it looked upon the swelling tide of business with an expression of complacency and half-disdain.

The house was not beautiful. There was nothing in its straight front of chocolate-coloured stone, its heavy cornices, its broad, staring windows of plate glass, its carved and bronze-bedecked mahogany doors at the top of the wide stoop, to charm the eye or fascinate the imagination. But it was eminently respectable, and in its way imposing. It seemed to say that the glittering shops of the jewellers, the milliners, the confectioners, the florists, the picture-dealers, the furriers, the makers of rare and costly antiquities, retail traders in the luxuries of life, were beneath the notice of a house that had its foundations in the high finance, and was built literally and figuratively in the shadow of St. Petronius' Church.

At the same time there was something self-pleased and congratulatory in the way in which the mansion held its own amid the changing neighbourhood. It almost seemed to be lifted up a little, among the tall buildings near at hand, as if it felt the rising value of the land on which it stood.

John Weightman was like the house into which he had built himself thirty years ago, and in which his ideals and ambitions were incrusted. He was a self-made man. But in making himself he had chosen a highly esteemed pattern and worked according to the approved rules. There was nothing irregular, questionable, flamboyant about him. He was solid, correct, and justly successful.

His minor tastes, of course, had been carefully kept up to date. At the proper time, pictures by the Barbizon masters, old English plate and portraits, bronzes by Barye and marbles by Rodin, Persian carpets and Chinese porcelains, had been introduced to the mansion. It contained a Louis Quinze reception-room, an Empire drawing-room, a Jacobean dining-room, and various apartments dimly reminiscent of the styles of furniture affected by deceased monarchs. That the hallways were too short for the historic perspective did not make much difference. American decorative art is *capable de tout*[1], it absorbs all periods. Of each period Mr. Weightman wished to have something of the best. He understood its value, present as a certificate, and prospective as an investment.

It was only in the architecture of his town house that he remained conservative, immovable, one might almost say Early-Victorian-Christian. His country house at Dulwich-on-the-Sound was a palace of the Italian Renaissance. But in town he adhered to an architecture which had moral associations, the Nineteenth-Century-Brownstone epoch. It was a symbol of his social position, his religious doctrine, and even, in a way, of his business creed.

"A man of fixed principles," he would say, "should express them in the looks of his house. New York changes its domestic architecture too rapidly. It is like divorce. It is not dignified. I don't like it. Extravagance and fickleness are advertised in most of these new houses. I wish to be known for different qualities. Dignity and prudence are the things that people trust. Every one knows that I can afford to live in the house that suits me. It is a

---

[1] Capable of anything.

guarantee to the public. It inspires confidence. It helps my influence. There is a text in the Bible about 'a house that hath foundations.' That is the proper kind of a mansion for a solid man."

Harold Weightman had often listened to his father discoursing in this fashion on the fundamental principles of life, and always with a divided mind. He admired immensely his father's talents and the single-minded energy with which he improved them. But in the paternal philosophy there was something that disquieted and oppressed the young man, and made him gasp inwardly for fresh air and free action.

At times, during his college course and his years at the law school, he had yielded to this impulse and broken away—now toward extravagance and dissipation, and then, when the reaction came, toward a romantic devotion to work among the poor. He had felt his father's disapproval for both of these forms of imprudence; but it was never expressed in a harsh or violent way, always with a certain tolerant patience, such as one might show for the mistakes and vagaries of the very young. John Weightman was not hasty, impulsive, inconsiderate, even toward his own children. With them, as with the rest of the world, he felt that he had a reputation to maintain, a theory to vindicate. He could afford to give them time to see that he was absolutely right.

One of his favourite Scripture quotations was, "Wait on the Lord." He had applied it to real estate and to people, with profitable results.

But to human persons the sensation of being waited for is not always agreeable. Sometimes, especially with the young, it produces a vague restlessness, a dumb resentment, which is increased by the fact that one can hardly explain or justify it. Of this John Weightman was not conscious. It lay beyond his horizon. He did not take it into account in the plan of life which he made for himself and for his family as the sharers and inheritors of his success.

"Father plays us," said Harold, in a moment of irritation, to his mother, "like pieces in a game of chess."

"My dear," said that lady, whose faith in her husband was religious, "you ought not to speak so impatiently. At least he wins the game. He is one of the most respected men in New York. And he is very generous, too."

"I wish he would be more generous in letting us be ourselves," said the young man. "He always has something in view for us and expects to move us up to it."

"But isn't it always for our benefit?" replied his mother. "Look what a position we have. No one can say there is any taint on our money. There are no rumours about your father. He has kept the laws of God and of man. He has never made any mistakes."

Harold got up from his chair and poked the fire. Then he came back to the ample, well-gowned, firm-looking lady, and sat beside her on the sofa. He took her hand gently and looked at the two rings—a thin band of gold, and a small solitaire diamond—which kept their place on her third finger in modest dignity, as if not shamed, but rather justified, by the splendour of the emerald which glittered beside them.

"Mother," he said, "you have a wonderful hand, and father made no mistake when he won you. But are you sure he has always been so inerrant?"

"Harold," she exclaimed, a little stiffly, "what do you mean? His life is an open book."

"Oh," he answered, "I don't mean anything bad, mother dear. I know the governor's life is an open book—a ledger, if you like, kept in the best book-keeping hand, and always ready for inspection—every page correct, and showing a handsome balance. But isn't it a mistake not to allow us to make our own mistakes, to learn for ourselves, to live our own lives? Must we be always working for 'the balance,' in one thing or another? I want to be myself,—to get outside of this everlasting, profitable 'plan,'—to let myself go, and lose myself for a while at least,—to do the things that I want to do, just because I want to do them."

"My boy," said his mother, anxiously, "you are not going to do anything wrong or foolish? You know the falsehood of that old proverb about wild oats."

He threw back his head and laughed. "Yes, mother," he answered, "I know it well enough. But in California, you know, the wild oats are one of the most valuable crops. They grow all over the hillsides and keep the cattle and the horses alive. But that wasn't what I meant—to sow wild oats. Say to pick wild flowers, if you like, or even to chase wild geese—to do something that seems good to me just for its own sake, not for the sake of wages of one kind or another. I feel like a hired man, in the service of this magnificent mansion—say in training for father's place as major-domo. I'd like to get out some way, to feel free—perhaps to do something for others."

The young man's voice hesitated a little. "Yes, it sounds like cant, I know, but sometimes I feel as if I'd like to do some good in the world, if father only wouldn't insist upon God's putting it into the ledger."

His mother moved uneasily, and a slight look of bewilderment came into her face.

"Isn't that almost irreverent?" she asked. "Surely the righteous must have their reward. And your father is good. See how much he gives to all the established charities, how many things he has founded. He's always thinking of others, and planning for them. And surely, for us he does everything. How well he has planned this trip to Europe for me and the girls—the court-presentation at Berlin, the season on the Riviera, the visits in England with the Plumptons and the Halverstones. He says Lord Halverstone has the finest old house in Sussex, pure Elizabethan, and all the old customs are kept up, too—family prayers every morning for all the domestics. By-the-way, you know his son Bertie, I believe."

Harold smiled a little to himself as he answered: "Yes, I fished at Catalina Island last June with the Honorable Ethelbert; he's rather a decent chap, in spite of his in-growing mind. But you?—mother, you are simply magnificent! You are father's masterpiece." The young man leaned over to kiss her, and went up to the Riding Club for his afternoon canter in the Park.

So it came to pass, early in December, that Mrs. Weightman and her two daughters sailed for Europe, on their serious pleasure trip, even as it had been written in the book of Providence; and John Weightman, who had made the entry, was left to pass the rest of the winter with his son and heir in the brownstone mansion.

They were comfortable enough. The machinery of the massive establishment ran as smoothly as a great electric dynamo. They were busy enough, too. John Weightman's plans and enterprises were complicated, though his principle of action was always simple—to get good value for every expenditure and effort. The banking-house of which he was the brain, the will, the absolutely controlling hand, was so admirably organised that the details of its direction took but little time. But the scores of other interests that radiated from it and were dependent upon it,—or perhaps it would be more accurate to say, that contributed to its solidity and success,—the many investments, industrial, political, benevolent, reformatory, ecclesiastical, that had made the name of Weightman well known and potent in city, church, and state, demanded much attention and careful steering, in order that each might produce the desired result. There were board meetings of corporations and hospitals, conferences in Wall Street and at Albany, consultations and committee meetings in the brownstone mansion.

For a share in all this business and its adjuncts John Weightman had his son in training in one of the famous law firms of the city; for he held that banking itself is a simple affair, the only real difficulties of finance are on its legal side. Meantime he wished the young man to meet and know the men with whom he would have to deal when he became a partner in the house. So a couple of dinners were given in the mansion during December, after which the father called his son's attention to the fact that over a hundred million dollars had sat around the board.

But on Christmas Eve father and son were dining together without guests, and their talk across the broad table, glittering with silver and cut glass, and softly lit by shaded candles, was intimate, though a little slow at times. The elder man was in rather a rare mood, more expansive and confidential than usual; and, when the coffee was brought in and they were left alone, he talked more freely of his personal plans and hopes than he had ever done before.

"I feel very grateful to-night," said he, at last; "it must be something in the air of Christmas that gives me this feeling of thankfulness for the many mercies that have been bestowed upon me. All the principles by which I have tried to guide my life have been justified. I have never made the value of this salted almond by anything that the courts would not uphold, at least in the long run, and yet—or wouldn't it be truer to say and therefore?—my affairs have been wonderfully prospered. There's a great deal in that text 'Honesty is the best'—but no, that's not from the Bible, after all, is it? Wait a moment; there is something of that kind, I know."

"May I light a cigar, father," said Harold, turning away to hide a smile, "while you are remembering the text?"

"Yes, certainly," answered the elder man, rather shortly; "you know I don't dislike the smell. But it is a wasteful, useless habit, and therefore I have never practised it. Nothing useless is worth while, that's my motto—nothing that does not bring a reward. Oh, now I recall the text, 'Verily I say unto you, they have their reward.' I shall ask Doctor Snodgrass to preach a sermon on that verse some day."

"Using you as an illustration?"

"Well, not exactly that; but I could give him some good material from my own experience to prove the truth of Scripture. I can honestly say that there is not one of my charities that has not brought me in a good return, either in the increase of influence, the building up of credit, or the association with substantial people. Of course you have to be careful how you give, in order to secure the best results—no indiscriminate giving—no pennies in beggars' hats! It has been one of my principles always to use the same kind of judgment in charities that I use in my other affairs, and they have not disappointed me."

"Even the check that you put in the plate when you take the offertory up the aisle on Sunday morning?"

"Certainly; though there the influence is less direct; and I must confess that I have my doubts in regard to the collection for Foreign Missions. That always seems to me romantic and wasteful. You never hear from it in any definite way. They say the missionaries have done a good deal to open the way for trade; perhaps—but they have also gotten us into commercial and political difficulties. Yet I give to them—a little—it is a matter of conscience with me to identify myself with all the enterprises of the Church; it is the mainstay of social order and a prosperous civilisation. But the best forms of benevolence are the well-established, organised ones here at home, where people can see them and know what they are doing."

"You mean the ones that have a local habitation and a name."

"Yes; they offer by far the safest return, though of course there is something gained by contributing to general funds. A public man can't afford to be without public spirit. But on the whole I prefer a building, or an endowment. There is a mutual advantage to a good name and a good institution in their connection in the public mind. It helps them both. Remember that, my boy. Of course at the beginning you will have to practise it in a small way; later, you will have larger opportunities. But try to put your gifts where they can be identified and do good all around. You'll see the wisdom of it in the long run."

"I can see it already, sir, and the way you describe it looks amazingly wise and prudent. In other words, we must cast our bread on the waters in large loaves, carried by sound ships marked with the owner's name, so that the return freight will be sure to come back to us."

The father laughed, but his eyes were frowning a little as if he suspected something irreverent under the respectful reply.

"You put it humourously, but there's sense in what you say. Why not? God rules the sea; but He expects us to follow the laws of navigation and commerce. Why not take good care of your bread, even when you give it away?"

"It's not for me to say why not—and yet I can think of cases—" The young man hesitated for a moment. His half-finished cigar had gone out. He rose and tossed it into the fire, in front of which he remained standing—a slender, eager, restless young figure, with a touch of hunger in the fine face, strangely like and unlike the father, at whom he looked with half-wistful curiosity.

"The fact is, sir," he continued, "there is such a case in my mind now. So I thought of speaking to you about it to-night. You remember Tom Rollins, the Junior who was so good to me when I entered college?"

The father nodded. He remembered very well indeed the annoying incidents of his son's first escapade, and how Rollins had stood by him and helped to avoid a public disgrace, and how a close friendship had grown between the two boys, so different in their fortunes.

"Yes," he said, "I remember him. He was a promising young man. Has he succeeded?"

"Not exactly—that is, not yet. His business has been going rather badly. He has a wife and little baby, you know. And now he has broken down,—something wrong with his lungs. The doctor says his only chance is a year or eighteen months in Colorado. I wish we could help him."

"How much would it cost?"

"Three or four thousand, perhaps, as a loan."

"Does the doctor say he will get well?"

"A fighting chance—the doctor says."

The face of the older man changed subtly. Not a line was altered, but it seemed to have a different substance, as if it were carved out of some firm imperishable stuff.

"A fighting chance," he said, "may do for a speculation, but it is not a good investment. You owe something to young Rollins. Your grateful feeling does you credit. But don't overwork it. Send him three or four hundred, if you like. You'll never hear from it again, except in the letter of thanks. But for Heaven's sake don't be sentimental. Religion is not a matter of sentiment; it's a matter of principle."

The face of the younger man changed now. But instead of becoming fixed and graven, it seemed to melt into life. His nostrils quivered with quick breath, his lips were curled.

"Principle!" he said. "You mean principal—and interest too. Well, sir, you know best whether that is religion or not. But if it is, count me out, please. Tom saved me from going to the devil, six years ago; and I'll be damned if I don't help him to the best of my ability now."

John Weightman looked at his son steadily. "Harold," he said at last, "you know I dislike violent language, and it never has any influence with me. If I could honestly approve of this proposition of yours, I'd let you have the money; but I can't; it's extravagant and useless. But you have your Christmas check for a thousand dollars coming to you to-morrow. You can use it as you please. I never interfere with your private affairs."

"Thank you," said Harold. "Thank you very much! But there's another private affair. I want to get away from this life, this town, this house. It stifles me. You refused last summer when I asked you to let me go up to Grenfell's Mission on the Labrador. I could go now, at least as far as the Newfoundland Station. Have you changed your mind?"

"Not at all. I think it is an exceedingly foolish enterprise. It would interrupt the career that I have marked out for you."

"Well, then, here's a cheaper proposition. Algy Vanderhoof wants me to join him on his yacht with—well, with a little party—to cruise in the West Indies. Would you prefer that?"

"Certainly not! The Vanderhoof set is wild and godless—I do not wish to see you keeping company with fools who walk in the broad and easy way that leads to perdition."

"It is rather a hard choice," said the young man, with a short laugh, turning toward the door. "According to you there's very little difference—a fool's paradise or a fool's hell! Well, it's one or the other for me, and I'll toss up for it to-night: heads, I lose; tails, the devil wins. Anyway, I'm sick of this, and I'm out of it."

"Harold," said the older man (and there was a slight tremor in his voice), "don't let us quarrel on Christmas Eve. All I want is to persuade you to think seriously of the duties and responsibilities to which God has called you. Don't speak lightly of heaven and hell. Remember, there is another life."

The young man came back and laid his hand upon his father's shoulder.

"Father," he said, "I want to remember it. I try to believe in it. But somehow or other, in this house, it all seems unreal to me. No doubt all you say is perfectly right and wise. I don't venture to argue against it, but I can't feel it—that's all. If I'm to have a soul, either to lose or to save, I must really live. Just now neither the present nor the future means anything to me. But surely we won't quarrel. I'm very grateful to you, and we'll part friends. Good-night, sir."

The father held out his hand in silence. The heavy portiere dropped noiselessly behind the son, and he went up the wide, curving stairway to his own room.

Meantime John Weightman sat in his carved chair in the Jacobean dining-room. He felt strangely old and dull. The portraits of beautiful women by Lawrence and Reynolds and Raeburn, which had often seemed like real company to him, looked remote and uninteresting. He fancied something cold and almost unfriendly in their expression, as if they were staring through him or beyond him. They cared nothing for his principles, his hopes, his disappointments, his successes; they belonged to another world, in which he had no place. At this he felt a vague resentment, a sense of discomfort that he could not have defined or explained. He was used to being considered, respected, appreciated at his full value in every region, even in that of his own dreams.

Presently he rang for the butler, telling him to close the house and not to sit up, and walked with lagging steps into the long library, where the shaded lamps were burning. His eye fell upon the low shelves full of costly books, but he had no desire to open them. Even the carefully chosen pictures that hung above them seemed to have lost their attraction. He paused for a moment before an idyll of Corot—a dance of nymphs around some forgotten altar in a vaporous glade—and looked at it curiously. There was something rapturous and serene about the picture, a breath of spring-time in the misty trees, a harmony of joy in the dancing figures, that wakened in him a feeling of half pleasure and half envy. It represented something that he had never known in his calculated, orderly life. He was dimly mistrustful of it.

"It is certainly very beautiful," he thought, "but it is distinctly pagan; that altar is built to some heathen god. It does not fit into the scheme of a Christian life. I doubt whether it is consistent with the tone of my house. I will sell it this winter. It will bring three or four times what I paid for it. That was a good purchase, a very good bargain."

He dropped into the revolving chair before his big library table. It was covered with pamphlets and reports of the various enterprises in which he was interested. There was a pile of newspaper clippings in which his name was mentioned with praise for his sustaining power as a pillar of finance, for his judicious benevolence, for his support of wise and prudent reform movements, for his discretion in making permanent public gifts—"the Weightman Charities," one very complaisant editor called them, as if they deserved classification as a distinct species.

He turned the papers over listlessly. There was a description and a picture of the "Weightman Wing of the Hospital for Cripples," of which he was president; and an article on the new professor in the "Weightman Chair of Political Jurisprudence" in Jackson University, of which he was a trustee; and an illustrated account of the opening of the "Weightman Grammar-School" at Dulwich-on-the-Sound, where he had his legal residence for purposes of taxation.

This last was perhaps the most carefully planned of all the Weightman Charities. He desired to win the confidence and support of his rural neighbours. It had pleased him much when the local newspaper had spoken of him as an ideal citizen and the logical candidate for the Governorship of the State; but upon the whole it seemed to him wiser to keep out of active politics. It would be easier and better to put Harold into the running, to have him sent to the Legislature from the Dulwich district, then to the national House, then to the Senate. Why not? The Weightman interests were large enough to need a direct representative and guardian at Washington.

But to-night all these plans came back to him with dust upon them. They were dry and crumbling like forsaken habitations. The son upon whom his complacent ambition had rested had turned his back upon the mansion of his father's hopes. The break might not be final; and in any event there would be much to live for; the fortunes of the family would be secure. But the zest of it all would be gone if John Weightman had to give up the assurance of perpetuating his name and his principles in his son. It was a bitter disappointment, and he felt that he had not deserved it.

He rose from the chair and paced the room with leaden feet. For the first time in his life his age was visibly upon him. His head was heavy and hot, and the thoughts that rolled in it were confused and depressing. Could it be that he had made a mistake in the principles of his existence? There was no argument in what Harold had said, it was almost childish, and yet it had shaken the elder man more deeply than he cared to show. It held a silent attack which touched him more than open criticism.

Suppose the end of his life were nearer than he thought—the end must come sometime—what if it were now? Had he not founded his house upon a rock? Had he not kept the Commandments? Was he not, "touching the law, blameless"? And beyond this, even if there were some faults in his character—and all men are sinners—yet he surely believed in the saving doctrines of religion—the forgiveness of sins, the resurrection of the body, the life everlasting. Yes, that was the true source of comfort, after all. He would read a bit in the Bible, as he did every night, and go to bed and to sleep.

He went back to his chair at the library table. A strange weight of weariness rested upon him, but he opened the book at a familiar place, and his eyes fell upon the verse at the bottom of the page.

> *"Lay not up for yourselves treasures upon earth."*

That had been the text of the sermon a few weeks before. Sleepily, heavily, he tried to fix his mind upon it and recall it. What was it that Doctor Snodgrass had said? Ah, yes—that it was a mistake to pause here in reading the verse. We must read on without a pause—*Lay not up treasures upon earth where moth and rust do corrupt and where thieves break through and steal*—that was the true doctrine. We may have treasures upon earth, but they must not be put into unsafe places, but into safe places. A most comforting doctrine! He had always followed it. Moths and rust and thieves had done no harm to his investments.

John Weightman's drooping eyes turned to the next verse, at the top of the second column.

> *"But lay up for yourselves treasures in heaven."*

Now what had the Doctor said about that? How was it to be understood—in what sense—treasures—in heaven?

The book seemed to float away from him. The light vanished. He wondered dimly if this could be Death, coming so suddenly, so quietly, so irresistibly. He struggled for a moment to hold himself up, and then sank slowly forward upon the table. His head rested upon his folded hands. He slipped into the unknown.

II

How long afterward conscious life returned to him he did not know. The blank might have been an hour or a century. He knew only that something had happened in the interval. What it was he could not tell. He found great difficulty in catching the thread of his identity again. He felt that he was himself; but the trouble was to make his connections, to verify and place himself, to know who and where he was.

At last it grew clear. John Weightman was sitting on a stone, not far from a road in a strange land.

The road was not a formal highway, fenced and graded. It was more like a great travel-trace, worn by thousands of feet passing across the open country in the same direction.

Down in the valley, into which he could look, the road seemed to form itself gradually out of many minor paths; little footways coming across the meadows, winding tracks following along beside the streams, faintly marked trails emerging from the woodlands. But on the hillside the threads were more firmly woven into one clear band of travel, though there were still a few dim paths joining it here and there, as if persons had been climbing up the hill by other ways and had turned at last to seek the road.

From the edge of the hill, where John Weightman sat, he could see the travellers, in little groups or larger companies, gathering from time to time by the different paths, and making the ascent. They were all clothed in white, and the form of their garments was strange to him; it was like some old picture. They passed him, group after group, talking quietly together or singing; not moving in haste, but with a certain air of eagerness and joy as if they were glad to be on their way to an appointed place. They did not stay to speak to him, but they looked at him often and spoke to one another as they looked; and now and then one of them would smile and beckon him a friendly greeting, so that he felt they would like him to be with them.

There was quite an interval between the groups; and he followed each of them with his eyes as it passed along the ribbon of the road rising and receding across the wide, billowy upland, among the rounded hillocks of aerial green and gold and lilac, until it came to the high horizon, and stood outlined for a moment, a tiny cloud of white against the tender blue, before it vanished over the hill.

For a long time he sat there watching and wondering. It was a very different world from that in which his mansion on the Avenue was built; and it looked strange to him, but most real—as real as anything he had ever seen. Presently he felt a strong desire to know what country it was and where the people were going. He had a faint premonition of what it must be, but he wished to be sure. So he rose from the stone where he was sitting, and came down through the short grass and the lavender flowers, toward a passing group of people. One of them turned to meet him, and held out his hand. It was an old man, under whose white beard and brows John Weightman thought he saw a suggestion of the face of the village doctor who had cared for him years ago, when he was a boy in the country.

"Welcome," said the old man. "Will you come with us?"

"Where are you going?"

"To the heavenly city, to see our mansions there."

"And who are these with you?"

"Strangers to me until a little while ago; I know them better now. But I have known you for a long time, John Weightman. Don't you remember your old doctor?"

"Yes," he cried—"yes; your voice has not changed at all. I'm glad indeed to see you, Doctor McLean, especially now. All this seems very strange to me, almost oppressive. I wonder if—but may I go with you, do you suppose?"

"Surely," answered the doctor, with his familiar smile; "it will do you good. And you also must have a mansion in the city waiting for you—a fine one, too—are you not looking forward to it?"

"Yes," replied the other, hesitating a moment: "yes—I believe it must be so, although I had not expected to see it so soon. But I will go with you, and we can talk by the way."

The two men quickly caught up with the other people, and all went forward together along the road. The doctor had little to tell of his experience, for it had been a plain, hard life, uneventfully spent for others, and the story of the village was very simple. John Weightman's adventures and triumphs would have made a far richer, more imposing history, full of contacts with the great events and personages of the time. But somehow or other he did not care to speak much about it, walking on that wide heavenly moorland, under that tranquil, sunless arch of blue, in that free air of perfect peace, where the light was diffused without a shadow, as if the spirit of life in all things were luminous.

There was only one person except the doctor in that little company whom John Weightman had known before—an old book-keeper who had spent his life over a desk, carefully keeping accounts—a rusty, dull little man, patient and narrow, whose wife had been in the insane asylum for twenty years and whose only child was a crippled daughter, for whose comfort and happiness he had toiled and sacrificed himself without stint. It was a surprise to find him here, as care-free and joyful as the rest.

The lives of others in the company were revealed in brief glimpses as they talked together—a mother, early widowed, who had kept her little flock of children together and laboured through hard and heavy years to bring them up in purity and knowledge—a Sister of Charity who had devoted herself to the nursing of poor folk who were being eaten to death by cancer—a schoolmaster whose heart and life had been poured into his quiet work of training boys for a clean and thoughtful manhood—a medical missionary who had given up a brilliant career in science to take the charge of a hospital in darkest Africa—a beautiful woman with silver hair who had resigned her dreams of love and marriage to care for an invalid father, and after his death had made her life a long, steady search for ways of doing kindnesses to others—a poet who had walked among the crowded tenements of the great city, bringing cheer and comfort not only by his songs, but by his wise and patient works of practical aid—a paralysed woman who had lain for thirty years upon her bed, helpless but not hopeless, succeeding by a miracle of courage in her single aim, never to complain, but always to impart a bit of her joy and peace to every one who came near her. All these, and other persons like them, people of little consideration in the world, but now seemingly all full of great contentment and an inward gladness that made their steps light, were in the company that passed along the road, talking together of things past and things to come, and singing now and then with clear voices from which the veil of age and sorrow was lifted.

John Weightman joined in some of the songs—which were familiar to him from their use in the church—at first with a touch of hesitation, and then more confidently. For as they went on his sense of strangeness and fear at his new experience diminished, and his thoughts began to take on their habitual assurance and complacency. Were not these people going to the Celestial City? And was not he in his right place among them? He had always looked forward to this journey. If they were sure, each one, of finding a mansion there, could not he be far more sure? His life had been more fruitful than theirs. He had been a leader, a founder of new enterprises, a pillar of Church and State, a prince of the House of Israel. Ten talents had been given him, and he had made them twenty. His reward would be proportionate. He was glad that his companions were going to find fit dwellings prepared for them; but he thought also with a certain pleasure of the surprise that some of them would feel when they saw his appointed mansion.

So they came to the summit of the moorland and looked over into the world beyond. It was a vast green plain, softly rounded like a shallow vase, and circled with hills of amethyst. A broad, shining river flowed through it, and many silver threads of water were woven across the green; and there were borders of tall trees on the banks of the river, and orchards full of roses abloom along the little streams, and in the midst of all stood the city, white and wonderful.

When the travellers saw it they were filled with awe and joy. They passed over the little streams and among the orchards quickly and silently, as if they feared to speak lest the city should vanish.

The wall of the city was very low, a child could see over it, for it was made only of precious stones. The gate of the city was not like a gate at all, for it was not barred with iron or wood, but only a single pearl, softly gleaming, marked the place where the wall ended and the entrance lay open.

A person stood there whose face was bright and grave, and whose robe was like the flower of the lily, not a woven fabric, but a living texture.

"Come in," he said to the company of travellers; "you are at your journey's end, and your mansions are ready for you."

John Weightman hesitated, for he was troubled by a doubt. Suppose that he was not really, like his companions, at his journey's end, but only transported for a little while out of the regular course of his life into this mysterious experience? Suppose that, after all, he had not really passed through the door of death, like these others, but was walking in a vision, a living man among the blessed dead. Would it be right for him to go with them into the heavenly city? Would it not be a deception, a desecration, a deep and unforgivable offence? The strange, confusing question had no reason in it, as he very well knew; for if he was dreaming, then it was all a dream; but if his companions were real, then he also was with them in reality, and if they had died then he must have died too. Yet he could not rid his mind of the sense that there was a difference between them and him, and it made him afraid to go on. But, as he paused and turned, the Keeper of the Gate looked straight and deep into his eyes, and beckoned to him. Then he knew that it was not only right but necessary that he should enter.

They passed from street to street among fair and spacious dwellings, set in amaranthine gardens, and adorned with an infinitely varied beauty of divine simplicity. The mansions differed in size, in shape, in charm: each one seemed to have its own personal look of loveliness; yet all were alike in fitness to their place, in harmony with one another, in the addition which each made to the singular and tranquil splendour of the city.

As the little company came, one by one, to the mansions which were prepared for them, and their Guide beckoned to the happy inhabitant to enter in and take possession, there was a soft murmur of joy, half wonder and half recognition; as if the new and immortal dwelling were crowned with the beauty of surprise, lovelier and nobler than all the dreams of it; and yet also as if it were touched with the beauty of the familiar, the remembered, the long-loved. One after another the travellers were led to their own mansions, and went in gladly; and from within, through the open doorways, came sweet voices of welcome, and low laughter, and song.

At last there was no one left with the Guide but the two old friends, Doctor McLean and John Weightman. They were standing in front of one of the largest and fairest of the houses, whose garden glowed softly with radiant flowers. The Guide laid his hand upon the doctor's shoulder.

"This is for you," he said. "Go in; there is no more sickness here, no more death, nor sorrow, nor pain; for your old enemies are all conquered. But all the good that you have done for others, all the help that you have given, all the comfort that you have brought, all the strength and love that you have bestowed upon the suffering, are here; for we have built them all into this mansion for you."

The good man's face was lighted with a still joy. He clasped his old friend's hand closely, and whispered: "How wonderful it is! Go on, you will come to your mansion next, it is not far away, and we shall see each other again soon, very soon."

So he went through the garden, and into the music within. The Keeper of the Gate turned to John Weightman with level, quiet, searching eyes. Then he asked, gravely:

"Where do you wish me to lead you now?"

"To see my own mansion," answered the man, with half-concealed excitement. "Is there not one here for me? You may not let me enter it yet, perhaps, for I must confess to you that I am only——"

"I know," said the Keeper of the Gate—"I know it all. You are John Weightman."

"Yes," said the man, more firmly than he had spoken at first, for it gratified him that his name was known. "Yes, I am John Weightman, Senior Warden of St. Petronius' Church. I wish very much to see my mansion here. I believe that you have one for me. Will you take me to it?"

The Keeper of the Gate drew a little book from the breast of his robe and turned over the pages.

"Certainly," he said, with a curious look at the man, "your name is here; and you shall see your mansion if you will follow me."

It seemed as if they must have walked miles and miles through the vast city, passing street after street of houses larger and smaller, of gardens richer and poorer, but all full of beauty and delight. They came into a kind of suburb, where there were many small cottages, with plots of flowers, very lowly, but bright and fragrant. Finally they reached an open field, bare and lonely-looking. There were two or three little bushes in it, without flowers, and the grass was sparse and thin. In the centre of the field was a tiny hut, hardly big enough for a shepherd's shelter. It looked as if it had been built of discarded things, scraps and fragments of other buildings, put together with care and pains, by some one who had tried to make the most of cast-off material. There was something pitiful and shamefaced about the hut. It shrank and drooped in its barren field, and seemed to cling only by sufferance to the edge of the splendid city.

"This," said the Keeper of the Gate, standing still and speaking with a low, distinct voice—"this is your mansion, John Weightman."

An almost intolerable shock of grieved wonder and indignation choked the man for a moment so that he could not say a word. Then he turned his face away from the poor little hut and began to remonstrate eagerly with his companion.

"Surely, sir," he stammered, "you must be in error about this. There is something wrong—some other John Weightman—a confusion of names—the book must be incorrect."

"There is no mistake," said the Keeper of the Gate very calmly; "here is your name, the record of your title and your possessions in this place."

"But how could such a house be prepared for me," cried the man with a resentful tremor in his voice—"for me, after my long and faithful service? Is this a suitable mansion for one so well known and devoted? Why is it so pitifully small and mean? Why have you not built it large and fair, like the others?"

"That is all the material you sent us."

"What!"

"We have used all the material that you sent us," repeated the Keeper of the Gate.

"Now I know that you are mistaken," cried the man with growing earnestness, "for all my life long I have been doing things that must have supplied you with material. Have you not heard that I have built a school-house; the wing of a hospital; two—yes, three—small churches, and the greater part of a large one, the spire of St. Petro——"

The Keeper of the Gate lifted his hand.

"Wait," he said; "we know all these things. They were not ill done. But they were all marked and used as foundations for the name and mansion of John Weightman in the world. Did you not plan them for that?"

"Yes," answered the man, confused and taken aback, "I confess that I thought often of them in that way. Perhaps my heart was set upon that too much. But there are other things—my endowment for the college—my steady and liberal contributions to all the established charities—my support of every respectable——"

"Wait," said the Keeper of the Gate again. "Were not all these carefully recorded on earth where they would add to your credit? They were not foolishly done. Verily, you have had your reward for them. Would you be paid twice?"

"No," cried the man, with deepening dismay, "I dare not claim that. I acknowledge that I considered my own interest too much. But surely not altogether. You have said that these things were not foolishly done. They accomplished some good in the world. Does not that count for something?"

"Yes," answered the Keeper of the Gate, "it counts in the world—where you counted it. But it does not belong to you here. We have saved and used everything that you sent us. This is the mansion prepared for you."

As he spoke, his look grew deeper and more searching, like a flame of fire. John Weightman could not endure it. It seemed to strip him naked and wither him. He sank to the ground under a crushing weight of shame, covering his eyes with his hands and cowering, face downward, upon the stones. Dimly through the trouble of his mind he felt their hardness and coldness.

"Tell me, then," he cried, brokenly, "since my life has been so little worth, how came I here at all?"

"Through the mercy of the King"—the answer was like the soft tolling of a bell.

"And how have I earned it?" he murmured.

"It is never earned; it is only given," came the clear, low reply.

"But how have I failed so wretchedly," he asked, "in all the purpose of my life? What could I have done better? What is it that counts here?"

"Only that which is truly given," answered the bell-like voice. "Only that good which is done for the love of doing it. Only those plans in which the welfare of others is the master thought. Only those labours in which the sacrifice is greater than the reward. Only those gifts in which the giver forgets himself."

The man lay silent. A great weakness, an unspeakable despondency and humiliation were upon him. But the face of the Keeper of the Gate was infinitely tender as he bent over him.

"Think again, John Weightman. Has there been nothing like that in your life?"

"Nothing," he sighed. "If there ever were such things, it must have been long ago—they were all crowded out—I have forgotten them."

There was an ineffable smile on the face of the Keeper of the Gate, and his hand made the sign of the cross over the bowed head as he spoke gently:

"These are the things that the King never forgets; and because there were a few of these in your life, you have a little place here."

The sense of coldness and hardness under John Weightman's hands grew sharper and more distinct. The feeling of bodily weariness and lassitude weighed upon him, but there was a calm, almost a lightness in his heart as he listened to the fading vibrations of the silvery bell-tones. The chimney clock on the mantel had just ended the last stroke of seven as he lifted his head from the table. Thin, pale strips of the city morning were falling into the room through the narrow partings of the heavy curtains.

What was it that had happened to him? Had he been ill? Had he died and come to life again? Or had he only slept, and had his soul gone visiting in dreams? He sat for some time, motionless, not lost, but finding himself in thought. Then he took a narrow book from the table drawer, wrote a check, and tore it out.

He went slowly up the stairs, knocked very softly at his son's door, and, hearing no answer, entered without noise. Harold was asleep, his bare arm thrown above his head, and his eager face relaxed in peace. His father looked at him a moment with strangely shining eyes, and then tiptoed quietly to the writing-desk, found a pencil and a sheet of paper, and wrote rapidly:

"My dear boy, here is what you asked me for; do what you like with it and ask for more if you need it. If you are still thinking of that work with Grenfell, we'll talk it over to-day after church. I want to know your heart better; and if I have made mistakes——"

A slight noise made him turn his head. Harold was sitting up in bed with wide-open eyes.

"Father!" he cried, "is that you?"

"Yes, my son," answered John Weightman; "I've come back—I mean I've come up—no, I mean come in—well, here I am, and God give us a good Christmas together."

www.ingramcontent.com/pod-product-compliance
Lightning Source LLC
LaVergne TN
LVHW010952100826
845153LV00002B/203
9781640323001